DUMB
LUCK

DUMB
LUCK

Lesley Choyce

Red Deer PRESS

Published by Red Deer Press, A Fitzhenry & Whiteside Company
195 Allstate Parkway, Markham, ON, L3R 4T8
www.reddeerpress.com

Published in the United States by Red Deer Press, A Fitzhenry & Whiteside Company
311 Washington Street, Brighton, Massachusetts, 02135

Edited for the Press by Peter Carver
Cover and text design by Daniel Choi
Cover image courtesy of iStockphoto
Printed and bound in Canada

5 4 3 2 1

We acknowledge with thanks the Canada Council for the Arts, and the Ontario Arts Council for their support of our publishing program. We acknowledge the financial support of the Government of Canada through the Canada Book Fund for our publishing activities.

Canada Council   Conseil des Arts
for the Arts   du Canada

ONTARIO ARTS COUNCIL
CONSEIL DES ARTS DE L'ONTARIO

Library and Archives Canada Cataloguing in Publication
Choyce, Lesley, 1951-
     Dumb luck / Lesley Choyce.
ISBN 978-0-88995-465-6
     I. Title.
PS8555.H668D84 2011   jC813'.54   C2011-905854-5

Publisher Cataloging-in-Publication Data (U.S)
Choyce, Lesley.
     Dumb luck / Lesley Choyce.
[240] p. : cm.
Summary: Brandon DeWolfe, an 18-year-old lonely misfit just barely getting through school, does what almost everyone else just dreams of: he wins the lottery. Plunged into a world that is completely new to him, and without any real moral compass to follow, Brandon realizes it's a good idea to be careful what you wish for.
1. Self-esteem -- Fiction. 2. Adolescence -- Fiction. I. Title.
[Fic] dc22   PZ7.C5693Du   2011

ANCIENT FOREST™
FRIENDLY

Preserving our environment
Fitzhenry & Whiteside chose to print the pages of this book on recycled paper and saved these resources[1]:

energy	water	greenhouse gases	solid waste
15 million BTUs	63,762 L	1,695 kg	484 kg

37 trees were saved for our forests

Printed by **Webcom Inc.** on
Legacy Hi-Bulk Natural 100% post-consumer waste.

FSC
www.fsc.org

MIX
Paper from
responsible sources

FSC® C004071

[1]Estimates were made using the Environmental Defense Paper Calculator.

Luck never gives. It only lends.

— Swedish proverb

chapter**one**

It all started the day I fell out of the tree.

Yes, a tree. I loved climbing trees. Big trees. Tall trees. Difficult to climb trees. I'd been climbing trees for as long as I could remember. Even though I was now seventeen, I still had a thing about climbing high up into the branches of a good tree. It was two days before my eighteenth birthday. School had just started and I was hating it. I'd never been very good at school. I'd failed grade seven and had to repeat it, so I was a year behind everyone else my age.

Most kids my age were in their last year of high school, but I had two years to go before I could get on with my life—my real life. I guess you could say that September and school combined to make me feel depressed. This is why Kayla asked me if I wanted to climb this giant old oak tree she'd discovered in a field not far out of town.

In my home town of Greenville, it seemed like they were cutting down all the trees to make way for shopping centers and strip malls and wider roads. I had counted twelve trees that used to be my climbing trees cut down with chain saws—just in my neighborhood. Nobody but Kayla and I seemed to care. And I just figured it was all part of the bad luck that had been dogging me all my life.

But Kayla grabbed me after school, took one look at my face, and said, "Let's go climbing." I knew immediately what she meant.

So, while other kids from school went to the mall or hit the coffee shop or hung out in the park, toking up or otherwise looking for trouble, my best friend and I took the Number 12 bus to the end of the line and then we hiked through somebody's pastureland until we came to the most amazing tree I'd ever seen around here.

Kayla and I had been climbing trees together since we were five years old. Kayla was my friend. Not a girlfriend. Just a friend. But a good friend. She had a habit of calling me Brando instead of my real name, Brandon. Nobody did this but her. She was smarter than me, but you could tell she didn't think very highly of herself. Even at seventeen (and a year ahead of me at school), she dressed like a boy, never combed her hair or wore makeup, was a little overweight, and had no boyfriends. She had what they call on talk shows "low self-esteem." But she was a fearless climber.

The sunlight was sending these amazing knives of light through the branches of the huge tree. It was unreal. It was very difficult to get up to the first branch, which must have been ten feet off the ground. I gripped my hands together, then Kayla put her foot in and lunged upward until she grabbed onto the branch. Then she pulled herself up, wrapped her legs around the branch, and reached down. I took her hand and she hoisted me up. The girl was strong.

We were laughing and joking around as we climbed higher and higher. My September blues were gone. Kayla's self-esteem was improving by the minute. We were like little kids again and it seemed impossible that in two more days I'd be eighteen. If I wanted to, I could now vote and I could join the military. But I didn't want to do either of those things. Right then, all I wanted to do was climb trees for the rest of my life and forget about school, forget about the world, forget about whatever lay ahead in my life.

Kayla kept going higher and I kept following her. I'd never seen her so full of spirit and so happy. I don't know how high up we were, but we were way up there. I mean *way* up there, and the branch we were sitting on together swayed a bit in the wind. I didn't look down. We were both breathing kind of heavy.

And then she did the weirdest thing. She leaned over, took my head in her hands, and kissed me.

Not on the mouth. Just on the cheek.

It came as a complete shock to my system. Kayla had never ever done such a thing in all the years we'd been hanging out together. I think I stopped breathing.

I guess I must have let go of the branch and leaned a little. Just then a gust of wind shook the tree and, before I realized what was happening, I fell.

Oh, I'd fallen out of trees before. But not a tree like this.

I remember screaming on the way down. And Kayla shouting out my name.

I remember scraping my ear on a branch and hitting another big limb with my shoulder. I even remember the impact when I hit the ground. Chest first—knocking the wind out of me. And then my head immediately connected with something very hard.

And then it went black.

And that was when my luck began to change.

chapter*two*

Through most of my life, I (and everyone else) had considered me unlucky. I almost never won any games. I was not good at sports so I didn't go out for any teams. I had a habit of being at the wrong place at the wrong time. I showed up late when I should have been on time. I showed up on time when it would have been better to show up late. I ended up at the end of long lines. I lost things. I never had any spending money. I'd had a couple of crappy part-time jobs that I'd been fired from and, of course, no girlfriends.

Some of that was my own fault, I know. Some of it was bad luck.

So it seemed strange that the first thing the doctor in the hospital said to me when I woke up was this: "You are one lucky son of a bitch."

My head hurt like hell. "Ouch," I said out loud.

"Head hurt?" Doc asked. For some insane reason he was smiling.

"Yeah," I answered. He shook his head. He looked like he was about to laugh. "Sorry," he said. "I'm Dr. Yates. You're Brandon, right?"

"I think so," I said. Someone had a hammer going inside my skull.

"I hear you fell out of a tree."

"Yeah."

"Well, your head hit a rock. That will explain the discomfort you're feeling."

Discomfort was not the word. I also now realized that I had a serious pain in my shoulder and it hurt when I breathed. "I don't really remember much. How did I get here?"

"Ambulance. The paramedics told us it didn't look good. You were in pretty rough shape. We could talk about all this later if you like."

I took another breath—pain, but nothing I couldn't live with. The head was still pounding but I wanted to hear more.

"Maybe I should bring your parents in," Dr. Yates said. "They're just outside."

"No," I said. "Not yet." I really didn't want to see my parents just now. My dad would have that look. My mom would be ... well, Mom. "What do you mean by lucky?"

Dr. Yates grabbed an x-ray that was in a folder at the end of my bed and held it up to the sunlight coming into the room. I tried to focus on it. He pointed to a spot on the shadowy thing that was the image of my skull. "Right there. That's where you connected with the rock. If ever there was a bad location to take impact on the head, that would be the place."

"Just my luck," I heard myself say.

"But that's the thing. You were lucky. Your skull did fracture a bit but it somehow fractured so that it distributed the force of the impact and it didn't really do any lasting damage."

"But it still hurts like hell."

He waved his hand in the air as if it was nothing. "We'll get you some Tylenol. Didn't want to give you any heavy meds. We wanted you back with us and conscious. You've got a fractured skull, Brandon, and a concussion, but the good news is you will be one hundred percent okay in no time."

"My father always said I had a thick skull," I said and started to laugh, but could tell that if I laughed, everything would hurt worse. Still, it was starting to sink in. It was good to be alive.

"He was right, I guess," the doc said. He was still smiling and seemed to find me and my situation strangely amusing. And then he said this: "You are about the luckiest person I ever met. If I had your luck, I'd go out and buy a lottery ticket as soon as I was out of here."

It was a funny thing for him to say, but it stayed with me.

My mom was crying when she saw me. But then she cried a lot. She hugged me and that hurt, but I tried not to show it. After a minute, I could feel her warm tears seeping through the hospital gown. My dad looked very concerned at first. "You gonna be all right, Brandon?" he asked.

"Yeah, the doctor says I'll be fine."

He almost held back and, at first, I thought he wouldn't go there. But he did.

I watched his lips tighten and then he said, "What the hell were you thinking?"

I'd learned a long time ago not to answer his questions. Maybe it wasn't the smartest or safest thing in the world to be way up there in the branches of an old oak tree. But it made me happy.

And not a lot of things did.

That's when I remembered the kiss. And Kayla.

"Is Kayla here?" I asked my dad.

My dad just shook his head. He never liked Kayla. She had never been very polite to him and I knew she thought he was too pushy and bullheaded. But then she never had much in the way of social skills. And, of course, my dad didn't like most people anyway.

My mom stopped sobbing and looked at me.

"The doctor says I'm okay, really. Saved by a thick skull."

"That, I believe," my old man said.

"What about Kayla?" I asked my mom.

"She was here but they sent her home."

"She must have been the one to get me here. I was with her. We were way out of town."

"I know," my dad said. "Climbing trees, for God's sake. What are you? A moron? You're not ten years old anymore." His hands were in the air.

"I need to talk to Kayla," I said to my mom, trying to avoid my father's stare.

"I think you should rest," she said.

The head was still pounding, the shoulder and ribs sore, but I needed to hear the part of the story I didn't remember. How did she get help? How did I get here?

The doctor popped back in. "Family reunion going well?" he asked.

My father just glared at him.

"When can I go home?" I asked.

"I want to keep you overnight. Just in case. You can probably go home tomorrow morning. But I'd like you to take a couple of days off from school."

That made me smile. Yeah, a couple of days off from school. Just what the doctor ordered. Maybe my luck was changing after all.

chapter*three*

The hospital food was much better than I expected and I ate like a horse. I tried calling Kayla at her home but no one was answering. I tried her cell phone a couple of times but no luck there either. Her battery was probably dead. I was worried that she was blaming herself for what had happened. It *was* kind of her fault. What was she thinking? She'd never done anything like that before. We were just friends. Good friends don't kiss in trees.

I fell asleep with a dull, throbbing drum beat in my head and a feeling of pressure in my chest, but it was a good sleep and a sound one.

When I woke up the next morning, the first face I saw was hers. It was Kayla, smiling at me in the morning sunlight. Her hair was brushed and she looked somehow different. "Brando, I'm so sorry," she said. "It was all my fault."

No way could I be mad at her. "Forget it," I said. "Let's just forget it." I meant the kiss, but I didn't want to use the word.

"You all right?"

"Apparently I have one thick skull and some amazing luck."

"I am so glad. I thought you were going to die."

I laughed as if it was no big deal. She looked at me directly in the eyes just then and we held the look, but then she suddenly looked away and out the window. "No more climbing trees for me for a while," I said.

"I shouldn't have taken you so high."

"I shouldn't have lost my balance. Let's leave it at that." But I was dying to know the rest of the story. The part where I was unconscious and lying on the ground and what happened after that. "Kayla, how did I get here?"

"An ambulance," she said.

"I know that, but how did you get help for me way out there?"

"After you fell, I climbed down. You were breathing but not conscious. I started to lose it. I really did. I started to cry. I didn't know what to do. Then I pulled myself together and tried calling 911 on my cell phone. But I couldn't get a signal."

"We were pretty far out of town." I could tell she was having a hard time telling the story. She looked like she was ready to cry and I was beginning to see how hard this must have been on her.

"So I had to climb back up in the tree," she said.

"How?" I remembered how we had to help each other to get to the lowest limb the first time.

"I don't know. I just did. When I got back up, almost to where we'd been sitting, I finally got a signal and got through. It seemed to take forever for them to get there. But the ambulance drove out across the field to us. And I came back here with you. But you never woke up the whole time. It was the worst time of my life." She was crying now.

I touched her shoulder. "But I'm going to be okay. I'll be out of here today and I get to take some time off from school." I smiled at her and brushed back her hair. It felt smooth and soft in my hands and it felt good. "So it has a happy ending," I said.

But it was only the beginning.

chapter**four**

Before I left the hospital that day, Dr. Yates took a picture of him and me together with the x-ray of my skull beside my head. It was a very funny photo and he said he would email me a copy. "Just remember how lucky you are," were his final words.

Kayla had gone off to school and my mom drove me home and was doting on me all day. Later in the afternoon she said, "Tomorrow's your birthday. Do you want to do anything special?"

"Not really," I said. Truth was I wasn't all that excited about turning eighteen. I didn't feel like I could possibly be that old. I was still a kid. I didn't want to grow any older. And I sure didn't want more responsibilities. I didn't really know what I wanted out of life. Finish school, I guess, and get the hell out of there. Maybe go to trade school and become an electrician. My dad said electricians make good money and you could work your own hours if you wanted to. What I really wanted to be was an airplane pilot, but everyone knew I didn't have the smarts for that. Or the luck.

Who would want to hire an airplane pilot who was not very smart, one who got left back in school and, in his spare time, fell out of trees? No way could that ever happen.

So the birthday came and went. I stayed home from school. There was a cake and eighteen candles. My mom said she couldn't believe that her baby was now a man. Oh God. And my dad had a couple too many beers—in celebration of my birthday—and gave me a lecture about how life is not easy. He said, "It never was and never will be for people like us. So you just need to suck it up and get on with it."

The next day I still didn't go to school. I was still recovering but my head felt better. I was okay. But I was tired of hanging around my house, watching really stupid videos on the Internet, so I walked down to the corner store, a place called "Dave's Pit Stop," and bought some chips and a bottle of Pepsi. Over the counter, I noticed the sign that said: *This Week's Super-Lotto is Worth $3 Million.*

I'd never bought a lottery ticket in my life. I guess I could have, but legally you weren't supposed to be allowed to buy one until you turned eighteen.

And then I thought, *Guess who just turned eighteen?*

And I remembered what Dr. Yates had said.

No way.

But I was bored. I had five dollars left in my pocket. I picked up one of those little paper slips where you pencil in the numbers you want. I asked Dave, "How do you do this?"

Dave looked at me like I was stupid. "You never did one before?"

"No."

"You gotta be eighteen," he said. "They come around here checking on me sometimes. Can't sell smokes to kids. Can't sell 'em beer or lottery tickets."

"I know," I said. "I just had a birthday."

He shrugged like he could care less. "Well, you take the pencil and blacken in the little boxes—pick six numbers. Any six. Who knows? You might get lucky."

I picked my six numbers. 3, 12, 21, 29, 33, 41.

I paid Dave, who had not asked to see any ID after all. Dave slipped my piece of paper into a machine and handed me my first ever official lottery ticket. I stared at it. My chance to be a multi-millionaire. Yeah, right.

It was a Friday. The lottery draw was the next night. I stashed the ticket in my now-empty wallet and walked home, thinking, yeah, the weekend. Two days off from school already. Two more off and I wouldn't have to be sitting in a classroom until Monday morning. Not such a bad deal.

Nothing much happened that day. Or the next. My headaches were gone. Doc Yates had e-mailed the funny photo of me and him and the x-ray of my head. I printed it out and put it on my wall. I got a weird e-mail from Kayla:

Brando,

I realize I kind of made a mess of our friendship. I'll never do that again.

I promise. I just want us to stay friends. Happy belated birthday.
Kayla

What's with girls anyway? Yeah, she had kind of mucked things up by kissing me but I just wanted to forget it and get on with my so-called life. So I just e-mailed back:

K,
All is well. Pretend it never happened. And next time we go climbing, remind me to bring a parachute.
B

I honestly didn't know if I'd ever climb a tree again but, hey, you have to have a little fun in life.

My Saturday night was about as dull as a Saturday night could be. Dinner with a grumpy dad, who complained about his job selling used cars to people he referred to as "losers and dimwits." I helped my mom wash the dishes and listened to her complain about my dad and how unhappy she was with the old house we lived in. (Doesn't get much more exciting than that.) And then I holed up in my room and watched some reality shows on TV.

I guess I could have actually watched the lottery draw on TV but I had forgotten about the ticket. Instead, I watched a show about a very unhappy family that had let cameras come into their lives to show the world how unhappy they were. There was a lot of screaming and slamming doors and it made me feel like maybe I didn't have it so bad.

I almost went to bed. When I was taking off my pants, my wallet fell to the floor and the ticket fell out.

So I picked it up.

And I sat down at my desk and Googled the lottery site.

And there were the winning numbers. 3, 12, 21, 29, 33, 41.

chapter*five*

I felt dizzy and light-headed. My eyes went kind of funny and my throat went dry. Was the room actually spinning or was it me? This just wasn't possible.

No way.

So I Googled another site that also had the lottery winning numbers and I stared at them again: 3, 12, 21, 29, 33, 41.

I looked at the little yellow piece of paper in my hand.

No freaking way.

I wondered if I was dreaming. My hands were sweating now. I stood up and walked in a small circle around my room and looked at my lottery ticket and the screen again.

I checked a third site and then went back to the official lottery Web site. It all checked out.

I thought about calling Kayla but everything was swimming in my head. I had to think this through. How much was it? Three million dollars. Right. In a few days, I would have three million dollars. My life would be totally different. My heart was racing now.

It was eleven o'clock at night and I was, of course, wide awake. I hid the lottery ticket at the bottom of my sock drawer and I went for a walk.

I can't even remember much about the walk. I ran into some kids drinking from a bottle of wine who said something to me—some kind of insult. But it didn't stick. I remember almost walking out into the street in front of a car. The driver hit his horn and yelled something to me about being retarded. I just smiled. I remember coming across the stump of what was once one of my favorite trees to climb in the neighborhood and I thought that, one day, I'd start replanting trees in places where they'd been cut down.

And then I was back home. My mom had heard me leave. Although my dad was asleep, my mom was still up and wanted to know where I'd been.

"Walking."

"Everything okay?"

I guess I couldn't hold it in any longer. "Just hang on," I said, and ran up to my room to bring the ticket back down.

I held it out. "I won," I said.

She smiled. She didn't believe me.

I went over to her laptop and turned it on. "I really did," I said.

She smiled some more.

The computer screen lit up. "Check it out."

She checked it out.

"Oh, my God," she said, her hand over her mouth.

"Oh, my God," I repeated calmly.

And then she burst into tears.

Lo and behold, when Monday morning rolled around, I did not go to school yet again. I was in the car with my mom and dad, headed to the lottery headquarters. Nobody in my family was in a bad mood. Nobody was crying.

On the way there, I got a text message from Kayla:

BRANDO,
WHERE R U? U OK?
KAYLA

I texted back:

K,
I'M VERY OK. NEVER BETTER.
YULE NEVER BELEEVE WHAT HAPPENED!
STAY TUNED.
B

At first, the people at the lottery corporation were very, very formal. They took the ticket, scanned it with something, looked at my ID, checked some records, and finally a smiley-faced bald guy in a suit, named Bradley Sweet, came into the room.

"Congratulations," he said. "We were afraid you might not come forward so soon. Some people hang back for days, even weeks."

I didn't really know what he was talking about, but he just kept shaking my hand and patting my father on the back. And then they gave me one of those big-ass cardboard checks. Three million dollars made out in my name.

Pictures were taken. Reporters asked questions. At first I just kind of blathered away, saying stupid stuff that probably didn't make any sense. But then, when I got myself straightened out and tried to sound normal, I just ended up laughing so hard I couldn't stop. After that it was all a blur.

I was on the TV news that night. I was in the papers. There were all kinds of weird phone calls and we had to unplug the phone. I had a ton of e-mails but didn't look at any of them. I was rich and I was the king of the world.

I had the big-ass check in my room. It was just for show. The money was already in my bank account. Yesterday my savings account had $43.76 in it. Today it had $3,000,043.76. I could go to my online banking and just sit there staring at the numbers. What next?

I didn't have the foggiest clue. All I knew was that I was feeling damn good. I could wake up tomorrow morning and pretty much do whatever I felt like doing.

My room phone was unplugged and my cell phone was off, but at two in the morning, I lay sweaty and fidgety in my bed, so I called Kayla. She answered after only one ring. I told her the story.

"This is real?" she asked.

"It's real."

"What even prompted you to buy a lottery ticket?"

"I don't know. It was my first one."

"But why now?"

"Because I'd turned eighteen. Because I fell out of a tree." I had almost said, *because you kissed me and I fell out of a tree.* But I didn't.

What followed was one of those incomprehensible conversations that was made up mostly of one- and two-syllable words. And as I got more excited trying to tell her about all the possible things I could do in my life, she suddenly screamed in my ear (in a good way) and said, "You are so damn lucky, Brando, and it couldn't have happened to a nicer guy."

And I think it was the first time anyone had said something so positive about me. Not only was I a multimillionaire but I was (corny as this sounds) a nice guy. And I liked that.

But there was no sleep for me that night.

chapter*six*

No way was I going to school on Tuesday. I needed some more time on this. I had finally fallen asleep near dawn and woke up around noon. The first thing I saw was a squirrel on a branch of a tree outside my window. He was looking right back at me, curious, as if he, too, knew I'd won some big money. He seemed to be saying, "So, you're the lucky bastard."

I got up out of bed and looked at myself in the mirror and answered, "Yes, I am," out loud, but then suddenly felt rather silly.

And then a voice in my head slammed out a question. "Now what?"

Yeah, now what?

I laughed right at that lucky bastard in the mirror.

Downstairs, I discovered my dad had taken his second day off from work. No selling silver SUVs for him today. "Welcome back to the world of the living, Brandon," he said, lowering the newspaper he was reading. I knew he'd been sitting there in the kitchen all morning, waiting for me.

"Morning, Dad," I said.

My mom appeared as if on cue. "What would you like to eat?"

There were the usual options. None of which particularly appealed to me. I thought for a minute. "Let's order out for something," I heard myself say. "It's on me."

My father gave me his as-if look, but my mother shushed him before he could say anything. Ordering out for any kind of food in my father's book had always been considered frivolous and too expensive.

"Sure," my mom said. "What would you like?"

I thought for a long minute about what someone who was rich and famous would order out for on Tuesday around noon. But I hadn't a clue.

"I want the most expensive pizza we can buy," I said. "And I want everything on it. And I do mean everything."

My dad gave me a hard look. I gave that look right back at him. Then he dropped the paper on the table and slapped me on the back. "You want pizza, we'll call for pizza." But it was my mother who made the phone call.

I rubbed the sleep out of my eyes and the three of us sat there at the kitchen table.

"We need to talk," my father said.

"I know," I answered.

"We have to come up with a plan."

I didn't like the sound of the word, "we," but I let it go. I knew that something like this was coming. "I know that, too."

"I've been thinking of opening up my own car lot," my dad said, suddenly not sounding like my usually grumpy dad. "This would be my chance."

Technically, of course, the money was mine, not ours. Who was he, to start thinking about how to spend my money? I was going to blurt out something but I decided to keep my mouth shut. I knew what he could be like if I pushed the wrong buttons. It was beginning to sink in that I was going to have to learn some things about what it was like to have a pile of money. And I guessed it might have to start with my parents. I decided to sidestep my dad for a minute.

My mother had been hovering, standing by the sink, looking a little nervous. I turned to her. "What about you, Mom? What do you want?"

She looked at me and blinked a couple of times. "I want a dishwasher," she said. Then she swallowed hard and added, "and a new sofa for the living room." And then she seemed embarrassed to have said these things out loud.

This was all so weird. My mom had always wanted a dishwasher but my father, of course, had considered it extravagant. It was one of those family issues that never went away but surfaced from time to time and created tension. I realized I could suddenly snap my fingers and solve many of my family's biggest problems.

"Mom, let's get you the dishwasher today. And whatever furniture you want." That was easy enough.

My dad looked a little annoyed that I had addressed her first, but he tried not to show it. I turned to him. "I thought you hated the used car business," I said.

"I don't love it but it's what I know. I just hate having to work for some asshole who gets to keep most of the profit." My father was the world's expert on assholes who get rich while poor slobs like him work their butts off.

I decided that I would try to play this like I was wise beyond my years. "How much you reckon it would take to get this project off the ground?"

"Fifty should do it," he said, looking away from me toward the door, as if he was checking to see if the pizza guy had arrived.

Now, I'd be the first to admit I have trouble with numbers. Up until last Saturday night, I didn't even know how many zeros there were in three million. Now I knew there were six zeros and one big three. But I didn't know what "fifty" meant to my father. Certainly not fifty dollars.

"Fifty?" I asked.

"Yeah. Fifty thousand would allow me to lease some land, get some inventory, hire maybe one other guy."

Maybe my father's dream was to become the asshole who gets rich on the hard work of the poor slob he hired. But he was my father. I was trying to do the math in my head. Three mil, take away $50,000. A dent but only a small dent. "And this would make you happy?"

"All my life, I've dreamed of being self-employed. Having my own business." His voice was different now. He wasn't talking to me like I was his kid. He was telling me the truth. And I'd heard him fantasize about having his own business before. It was his dream.

"Then I think you should go for it," I said.

He reached out and gave me a high five, the first one he'd ever given me in my eighteen years of life. But it felt damn good.

We made small talk after that until the pizza arrived. My dad had to pay for it because I didn't have any cash.

The pizza did have everything on it. Way too much of everything. The anchovies did not work well with the pineapples. In truth, it was one of the crappiest pizzas I ever ate but I didn't say it out loud. And no one complained in our kitchen.

In the afternoon, we drove to the bank where I got myself a couple of credit cards. Then we went to the shopping center and picked out a dishwasher, a sofa, and a couple of overstuffed chairs for the living room. My mom was in heaven. On the way home, my father drove by a couple of potential properties for his car lot. Maybe I should have been feeling good about being able to help out my dad, but I still didn't know what I was going to do with *my* money and I wanted some time to think it through. Why did he always have to be so pushy? But, yet again, I kept my mouth shut.

I guess I was pretty quiet on the way home. "You still alive back there?" my dad asked, sounding lighter and happier than I'd ever heard him.

"Yeah, I'm still here." But I was somewhere else. I don't know where I was. I kept thinking I should come up with a list. What did *I* want?

A sweet car.

A dirt bike.

A big honking HD flat screen TV for my bedroom.

And a girlfriend.

Yeah, I really, really wanted a girlfriend.

chapter**seven**

Those photographs they took at the lottery headquarters ended up not only in the papers but all over the Internet. And there was that dumb interview I did for TV, where I stuttered a little and just laughed when the reporter asked me how it felt to be a winner. Somebody posted that on the Internet, too, with the title: *Losers Sometimes are Winners.*

I was getting a ton of e-mails from kids at school and from people I didn't even know. There were even e-mails from girls that included pictures. All my life I had wanted people to like me. I had wanted to be popular. And now. Bingo. Like magic. This was going to be the way my life would go from now on. I felt a warm glow all over.

The phones were all unplugged in the house so no one could

get through. I turned on my cell phone and saw two text messages from Kayla:

U ALRIGHT?
K

and

CALL ME.
K

So I called her on my cell phone, which had been off all day.

"Your home phone isn't working," she said, sounding a little miffed.

"I know," I said. "People kept calling. Weirdos wanting to congratulate me."

I heard Kayla take a deep breath. "Things are going to be different, aren't they?"

"What do you mean?"

"I mean with you. With us."

I guess I was still a bit thick. A bit overwhelmed by it all. "What do you mean, *us*?"

Kayla didn't answer. "When are you coming back to school?"

"I'll be there tomorrow," I said. "But I'm thinking of quitting." The words just kind of jumped out of me.

"Brando. Why would you quit school?"

"I always hated school. I was never good at it. Now I can just quit if I want to. Why bother staying?"

"But I thought you were going to finish high school and then train to be an electrician."

"But I don't have to do that now."

"Brandon, this is so unlike you." Now she sounded like she was lecturing me. I wondered why I had even bothered to call her.

I was feeling annoyed. And defiant. I don't know why. "Well, now everything *is* different. I'm different."

And she hung up on me.

When I got to school the next day, *everything* was different. My mom drove me there. She said maybe I shouldn't take the bus for my first day back. "Why don't I rent a limo?" I had said, smiling. But she just tapped me gently on the forehead with her knuckle. Point made.

So I got out of my mom's car and looked around the front of the school. Everyone was looking at me. Some young geeky kid ran up and took a picture of me with his cell phone. My mom drove off and I was left standing there with all those faces, those eyes turned in my direction. I had my books under my arm and a paper bag with my lunch in it. I don't know why, but it was the lunch bag that made me feel self-conscious. Me. I had three million dollars in the bank and I'm standing there in front of everyone with a ham sandwich that my mom had packed. How humiliating.

I tossed the bag into a trash can and headed for the school door. I waved to a couple of the guys I knew—Josh and Derek—who were madly waving back. And then I saw Taylor smiling at me. Taylor never smiled at me. She had never given me the time of day.

Taylor was Taylor—always attached to one cool guy or another, never for long. Taylor owned the male population of the school and could have any guy she wanted. Now she was smiling at me.

I smiled back.

Get real, I kept telling myself. You've just walked into a little fantasy world. You'll wake up soon. Taylor will have stopped smiling, the money will be gone. My head felt a little dizzy. Maybe this was some kind of hallucination. I had fallen out of a tree, after all.

The bell rang and everyone started heading in. There were kids all around me and I kept hearing my name.

"Yo, Brandon."

"Hey, Brand."

"How'd you do it, dude?"

"What's it feel like?"

"Hey, man, ya wanna hang out?"

Some of them I knew. Some were just faces from around school.

And then Kayla was alongside of me. She grabbed my arm. "Brandon, you look like you're about to faint."

"I'm a little dizzy."

"Sorry I hung up on you."

"I must have deserved it"

"Not really. I overreacted."

"No, you didn't. I heard myself. I sounded like an asshole."

"Well, maybe a little," Kayla admitted.

"Like my grandfather used to say, 'There's more horses' asses in the world than there are horses.'"

"Your grandfather really said that?"

"Yeah. It was his explanation for just about everything."

"I would have liked your grandfather," Kayla said, guiding me to my locker. I'd been away from school for a few days and everything did seem different. It was like unknown territory to me. And everyone kept looking at me. I was feeling pretty spaced.

At my locker, I swallowed hard and looked at Kayla. "What do I do?" I asked. "I'm not sure I know how to handle this." I really was nervous about all the attention. And it might only get more intense.

"Just be yourself."

"I'm not sure who that is anymore."

I looked at Kayla. We'd been friends for a long time.

She looked worried. "Just go to class. Try not to draw too much attention to yourself." She nodded at the masses swirling around us. "They can't help themselves. You're their hero now because you won."

Hero? What the hell had I done to be a hero? All I did was get lucky. Nonetheless, I found myself smiling at those who were walking by. Especially the girls who were eyeing me. This was too much. I smiled and nodded at the girls from some of my classes who probably hadn't even known my name until this past weekend. Smart girls. Hot girls. And there I was, standing by my locker with my pudgy-faced girl buddy who liked to climb trees.

That was when I discovered I could actually give eye contact back to some of those young women walking by. I mean real eye contact. I was beginning to think that I'd turned some kind of corner in my life. I had stayed away from school for a few days and returned to an alternate universe where Brandon the Invisible had turned into Brandon the Magnificent. Maybe I was going to like this after all.

chapter eight

Kayla followed me to my first class—English. She squeezed my hand and then rushed on down the hallway, late for her own math class. I was a little shocked at what was going through my brain right then. I even hate to admit it, but this is what I was thinking: *I'm going to have to ditch Kayla if I want some of those girls to come up and talk to me.*

Yep. That was the plan. At the time, I wasn't even thinking straight. I wasn't thinking about our friendship and the fact that she had saved my sorry ass when I fell out of the tree. I was just thinking about me. The new me.

Which is why I didn't notice where I was going. As I was walking down the aisle between the desks, Grant Freeman had his leg out. Maybe he did it on purpose. I don't know. But I tripped.

My books and papers went flying and I went down hard, smashing first into Brittany Michaels' desk, making her scream. Then a proper face plant onto the linoleum floor. Gravity was clearly not my friend these days.

Everyone laughed. They were laughing at me. Not that it was the first time. It's just that before I would have brushed myself off, felt embarrassed, and shuffled to my seat. But now, thanks to winning the money, well, like I said, I was starting to change.

I now had an ego. Or at least I was working on one.

A teenage male ego.

I didn't like being laughed at.

I wasn't going to take that crap any more.

I picked myself up and glared at Grant. And his grin said it all. He had done this on purpose.

And then I lost it. I grabbed his leg and yanked him out of his seat onto the floor. He recovered quickly and came up swinging, just as Mr. King was walking into the room. Sadly for Grant, Mr. King grabbed him by one arm and was pulling him backwards just as I let go my first honest punch in my entire life. Brandon the Magnificent had somehow turned into Brandon the Maniac.

I can't say I hit him hard. I wasn't a fighter. But I did connect with the bridge of his nose. And there was blood for my fellow English students to see. Grant let out a bellow. And poor Mr. King didn't know what to do but shout, "Back off, Brandon!"

As I backed off, I fell backwards onto Brittany's desk again and sent her books flying. I straightened myself and looked around at the other students. Some were laughing. Some looked shocked.

Some seemed just plain freaked. But Taylor was watching it all from the back of the room. She was just smiling that smile I'd seen earlier. And yes, there was eye contact.

Grant was trying to kick me as Mr. King now held both of his hands behind his back. Blood was dripping down the front of Grant's face and he spit some of it at me but missed.

I should have felt stupid or embarrassed or guilty or something like that. But I didn't. Grant was one of those guys I'd known since I was a little kid. Good at sports. Good looking. From a well-known family. Everyone thought he was the golden boy, but he had a way of making kids like me feel like shit. Silly little things he'd say to put them (or me) in my place. Adults never saw it, but those of my tribe knew he got his true joy from making losers like me feel small and insignificant.

Now this.

Mr. King was afraid to let go of Grant. He didn't know what to do. I felt a little sorry for him, but I realized I had a smirk on my face as I looked straight into the anger of Grant Freeman's eyes. Strange thoughts filtered through my brain. *What can they do to me? Kick me out of school? I don't even want to be here. I don't need to be here. I can walk out of here and do whatever I want for the rest of my life.*

They say money isn't everything. Maybe not. But the money had given me a newfound courage.

"Brandon," Mr. King finally shouted. "Go to the office. Go to Mr. Carver's office now."

I blinked at him at first, then watched some more blood drip from Grant's nose. Grant started to say something. It wasn't polite whatever it was. A threat. "I'm gonna ..." but at that point, he must have sucked in his breath and swallowed some blood. He started coughing.

I had been given my cue. So I slowly walked around him and Mr. King and took my time finding the door. I also took my time walking to the office. By the time I'd made it there, Mr. King must have reported that I was coming. Mrs. Klein watched me as I arrived and just pointed with a cocked thumb to the open door of Mr. Carver's office. "He's waiting for you," she said.

Joseph Carver was a guidance counselor and also the vice principal—the man who routinely dealt with problems at the school. He was black. And he was gay. Everyone knew he was gay. He was maybe forty years old. And he was one of the most likeable adults I'd ever met.

Mr. Carver looked up from some paperwork on his desk. He tipped his glasses up from the bridge of his nose. "Brandon De-Wolfe," he said. "Didn't you just win a whole shit-load of money?"

I nodded.

"Then what the hell are you doing getting into a fight with Grant Freeman, first thing in the morning?"

"He tripped me."

"Please close the door. I don't want Mrs. Klein listening in on this."

I closed the wooden door with a thud.

He let out an exasperated breath. "Sit down, please."

I sat.

"This isn't the third grade you're in, is it?"

"No. I guess not."

Mr. Carver leaned back in his chair and rubbed his forehead. "I read about you in the papers and my first thought was, this couldn't have happened to a nicer person."

"Thank you," I said. Funny, that was exactly what Kayla had said.

"But then I had second thoughts. I started to worry."

"What's to worry about? I just had some amazing luck."

"Luck is a two-edged sword," he said, readjusting his glasses.

"What do you mean?"

"I mean, here you are, sitting in my office. That only means one thing."

"I'm sorry about this morning."

"Sorry is an easy word. Too easy. Say you're sorry to Grant. Or don't, if you prefer. Grant probably did try to trip you. But you don't want enemies. Not now that you have luck. And money. How much was it?"

"Three," I said.

"Three," he repeated. "What on earth is a kid like you going to do with three million dollars?"

"I haven't exactly figured that out yet."

He leaned forward and looked into my eyes. "You know what I'd do if I won what you did?"

"Quit your job?"

He suddenly appeared animated. "Hell, no. I like my job. If I quit, what would I do with myself all day?"

"Go on a trip?"

"You go on a trip and then you go back home and then what?"

"But you could take it easy. Do whatever you want to do."

He threw his hands out. "That's what I'm doing now. That's my point. I'd keep doing my job. I wouldn't change much of anything."

"You like dealing with snotty teenagers? You like having to deal with people's problems?"

"Yes. I do. Life is all about problems and how we deal with them. Right now I'm dealing with you. And I never had to deal with you before. Not like this. And what I see is trouble with a capital T."

"I'll be okay. I think Grant was just jealous of my good luck. He never hardly paid attention to me before."

"Well, see. Now that you had your picture in the paper with that big cardboard check, all kinds of people are going to pay attention to you. You notice that yet?"

I nodded.

"And how are you gonna know who your friends are?"

"I'll know," I lied. "And I kind of like that people are looking at me differently now. I'm not invisible anymore."

"Girls?"

"Yeah. Girls."

"You do understand what they're thinking, don't ya? 'There's Brandon DeWolfe who just won the lottery. Wouldn't it be cool to have him for a boyfriend?' You think that's a good thing?"

I nodded. "Sure. It's nice to have the attention."

Mr. Carver just shook his head. "Capital T," was all he said. He turned around to the window and looked up at the way the flag was rippling in the wind. "Attention can be good or bad. Most of my life I've been a black man living in a very white community. So I get attention. And to top that off, I'm a gay man."

"You're gay?" I asked, just to see how he would react.

"Everyone in this school knows I'm gay. Don't mess with me."

I shrugged and smiled.

"So here I sit, a gay black man who is also a vice principal at a school. That draws attention. Do you follow me so far?"

I didn't really see the connection but I nodded.

"So people know I stand out for who I am and they aren't exactly offering me congratulations on account of being either black or gay. So I have to do my job very well and live my life the best I know how. And, let me tell you, it is not easy."

"But I'm not black and I'm not gay," I said a bit too flippantly.

Mr. Carver wrinkled his brow. "I think you may be missing the point. The point is you have garnered the world's attention. You didn't earn it. You didn't work for it. You walked into a corner store and put your money on the counter. Fate did the rest. Now you have to figure some shit out pretty damn quick or you're gonna end up in a mess."

Maybe if he'd said this in the way you'd expect a VP to say it, I wouldn't have even taken it seriously. But this was different. I was a little ticked off about this lecture now. What was his problem? Maybe he was jealous that he didn't win the lottery. He saw the look on my face and could tell I wasn't really taking him seriously.

Joseph Carver turned to his computer and worked the keyboard until he found what he wanted. "I'm gonna give you some homework. You do this and I'll forget about the fight. You'll still need to apologize to Mr. King. And to Grant. And you'll have to drop in from time to time."

His printer went into action and in a second, a single page was printed. Mr. Carver handed it to me. On the page was a list of names. "Look them up and tell me what you found," he said. "Now sit in the office until the bell rings. And then go to your next class. If Grant tries to draw you into something, walk away. Walking away is good, remember that. It takes focus and a strong will. You are gonna need both."

As I sat in the office and waited for the bell to ring, Mrs. Klein kept one eye on me. I sat quietly and studied the list of names—none of whom I had heard of.

chapter*nine*

On my way to second period, without Kayla in tow, two girls approached me. Brittany Michaels at first and then Jessica Firth. They both asked the same question: "What does it feel like?"

And I didn't have any easy answer. Confused is what I might have said, but also exciting. I was still kind of shy around both of them, but then Taylor ambushed me, rounding a corner as I bumped right into her. I'm sure she did this on purpose. Brittany and Jessica faded as I stood there chest to chest with Taylor. "I'm so sorry," she said. "My fault entirely."

"Sorry," I said as well and tried to step away but she wouldn't let me.

"Hold out your hand," she instructed. I couldn't believe I had just had a full frontal encounter with one of the most beautiful girls in the school. I'm sure I was blushing. I held out my hand. She held it with one hand and with the other took a marker and wrote her phone number on the palm of my hand. "Call me," she said. "I want you to tell me everything."

And then she turned and walked away. I stared in disbelief at the number she had written on my hand until I could eventually make my legs move and I walked off down the hall.

Nothing much of what any teacher said that day stayed with me. I started to get used to other kids staring at me. And I began to daydream about how my life would change. How it already was changing.

I'd like to tell you I had deep, serious thoughts about how I would use my good fortune to make the world a better place. But that wasn't the way it was. I thought about getting that dirt bike I wanted. A really hot Kawasaki. And a car. I didn't even have a driver's license yet but I would need a really nice car. Beyond that and some serious video games, it was all kind of foggy. What would I do with all that money? I didn't know.

Kayla was standing outside the door of my last class of the day and I have to admit, I wish she had left me alone. I couldn't just say that to her, though.

"I heard about Grant Freeman," she said.

"He did it on purpose to make me look stupid," I said. "I'm not going to let anyone make me look stupid again."

"Let it go," she advised.

"I'll try."

We walked along in silence for a while until a carload of girls beeped and waved. I waved back and Kayla just shook her head. After a serious intake of breath she said, "I'm gonna lose you, aren't I?"

"What do you mean?"

"This is going to change you."

"I'm still me. Nothing's changed but my luck and the amount of money in my bank account." But I was lying and I knew it.

Kayla stared straight ahead and said nothing. By the time I said goodbye to her, there was only silence between us. And a wall. I don't know why it bothered me so much, but it did. I tried to slough it off but it made me feel really bad.

To make matters worse, my parents were arguing when I walked in the door. I heard them really going at it and I didn't want to hang around. So I went back out, walked about ten blocks to my bank and withdrew $1,000. The teller didn't question me at all. Everyone knew who I was now. I wasn't just the kid with $40 in his savings account. I didn't even know what I was gonna do with the cash, but it felt pretty cool having this big wad of fifties in my pocket.

Hey, the sun was out. I was a rich dude and I could go in any store, buy anything I wanted, go anywhere I wanted. Call a cab on my cell phone if I liked. Hell, I could call a limo. I could do that.

But I didn't.

Instead, I went into a Starbuck's and bought a large cappuccino. I think the girl behind the counter recognized me. She smiled at me like the girls in school. I handed her a fifty, accepted the change and gave her a ten dollar tip. She smiled some more. When I sat down by the window, I looked at the phone number on my hand.

Nope. Not quite yet. If I was going to call Taylor, I couldn't sound all nervous and wimpy. I needed a bit more courage.

Sitting there in Starbuck's, alone at a small table in a pool of sunlight, I started to see all the possibilities ahead of me. I began to see everything that money could buy. Having money had always seemed unreal to me. My future had always been a fog bank. It still was. But the fog was clearing.

Back on the street, an old guy with an empty coffee cup asked me for money, and I said I'd give him a big tip if he'd go into the liquor store and buy me a small bottle of Jack Daniels. I'd had a few drinks before, nothing serious. A few beers here and there, some booze that I sneaked from my dad's liquor cabinet. I don't know what inspired me now but I remembered how booze had made me feel and I liked it. I handed the guy a twenty and I followed him to the liquor store, where he went in and came back out with a small bottle in a brown bag for me. He went to hand me back the change and I told him to keep it. He smiled.

"Thanks, buddy," he said. "That's the good stuff you got there." As I turned to go, I handed him another twenty. I was feeling generous. I tucked the bottle in my book bag and started to walk away, the big wad of bills still in my pocket. After a couple of blocks, I flagged down a cab and took the easy way home. It was only when I was sitting in the back of the cab that I remembered I was now eighteen and could have walked into that liquor store and legally bought the bottle of booze in my backpack.

chapter*ten*

My mom and dad were still arguing when I got home. They did that sometimes. My dad had a bad habit of being loud and my mother usually ended up crying. Often, I'd come home and my mom would have saved me some dinner, but tonight I decided to skip whatever was left of supper and head to my room to avoid the drama.

I stashed my bottle of courage in my desk and decided that tonight was not the night for a taste of the demon alcohol. I copied Taylor's phone number onto a piece of paper, still not quite believing she had given it to me. I was not ready to call her. I didn't even know what I would say to her. I could see her pretty face clearly in my head and my brain teased me with images of me and Taylor at a party together or, better yet, alone in a car somewhere.

Despite the fact that my father sold used cars and I was old enough to drive, he had often told me that I wasn't ready yet for the responsibility of driving. He said that even if I got a driver's license, I wouldn't be allowed to drive the family Acura and he wasn't willing to put up any money for the driving course I needed to take. That had really pissed me off, but I guess I never had the ambition to follow through anyway and get the license on my own.

But, of course, now everything was different. Or was it? I checked my inbox and discovered I had a ton of e-mails. Mostly from people I didn't know. How did that happen? Somehow people had found out my e-mail address. I opened a couple. One was from a man whose name was Ron, who said his son was dying of a rare form of cancer and that he needed to fly the boy to India for a treatment not available here. He said it was the only way to save his son. He included his phone number and begged for me to call him. A chill ran down my spine.

Another one was from a young woman. She included a picture. She must have been in her early twenties. And she was quite sexy. She was asking me for money, too. This time for "cosmetic surgery," but she didn't say what kind. She also said that she would make it worth my while if I did this, and she would be most grateful.

I swallowed and looked at her picture again, but then clicked back to my inbox.

I didn't recognize any of the names of people sending messages.

The first few days after winning the lottery were a bit of a daze to me, but today was something different. Now I was seeing that I had suddenly come into focus for everyone around me. For so long, almost no one had really paid much attention to me. And now this. I wasn't completely sure I was liking everything about my new life. Not the way people treated me. Not even the way I was beginning to see the world around me. I thought about the man with the sick kid. Why not just call him up and give him what he needed? But what about all the others who would come looking for me to help?

Maybe I should just give all the money away, I thought for the first time.

Oh, hell. I was tired of thinking about it. And I was hungry. I decided to take a chance and head down to the kitchen.

My mom had gone to her room, but my dad was sitting there with the laptop and some papers spread out around him. He appeared a bit frazzled, but then my dad often looked frazzled. He looked up at me and smiled, but it was his car salesman smile, not the smile of the father who used to play catch with me when I was little.

"How was school, Brandon?"

"Different," I said, keeping things purposely vague.

"Welcome to the world of the rich and famous." He looked back at his computer screen. "Wanna take a look at this?"

I looked. It was an empty city lot, a field full of weeds. "What am I looking at?"

"The future," he said.

I didn't get it.

"The future site of my business," he explained.

"Why there?"

"Location, Brandon. It's all about location. It's on the highway, halfway between two of the biggest used car dealerships in the city. And because they are big and I'll be small—at least I'll start out small—then I'll have much lower overhead. I can sell the same model cars they're selling for at least ten percent less. Any smart consumer will end up buying from me."

Maybe I should have been excited for him because I could see he was excited in a good way. And I didn't see him like that very often. He could do this, I began to realize, because I would be putting up the money. Sure. Why not? But then I began to wonder: was I loaning him the money or giving him the money? I decided that now was not the time to ask.

"Any leftovers?" I asked.

"There's chicken in the fridge. Some potatoes and peas, too. Put some on a plate and pop it into the microwave." He wasn't about to get up and get me dinner, I could see.

So I sliced off some chicken, scooped some mashed potatoes on a plate and threw it into the microwave, thinking the headline would read: *Millionaire Son Forced to Reheat Leftover Chicken for Dinner.* Maybe nothing had really changed at all. After a couple of minutes, I sat down to eat at the table with my dad. "What were you and mom fighting about?"

He didn't look up from his computer where he was scrolling through images of cars for sale. "You know how she gets."

I knew she was overly emotional sometimes. Well, lots of times, but it still wasn't an answer. "What got her going this time?"

Now he looked up. "I quit my job."

I hadn't seen that coming. "You what?"

"Yeah. I quit. If I'm gonna do this thing right, I need to put everything into it."

"Oh, shit," I said out loud. What was he thinking? I didn't like the way that everything was changing so quickly. And that he was all ready to make such a big gamble with my money. "That was stupid," I told him outright.

I thought he was going to lose it then. I had never called him stupid before. He was about to say something, but he stopped himself and gave me a look that drilled right through me.

"Well, I thought you'd take this one step at a time," I added, backing off a bit.

"I am. And the first step is to get the down payment on that land you looked at, get the sucker paved, and move a nicely appointed trailer onto there. Brandon, you're the dude who is making this all possible."

Dude? My uptight father called me *dude*? "But it seems a bit quick."

"Hey, the money is in the bank. It's just sitting there getting— what?—two percent interest."

I suddenly wanted to say, "But it's my money." But I didn't. My father read the look on my face. "Brandon, I thought a lot about this. This is my big chance. And I thought about you. Sure, I'm your father, but you don't owe me anything. I remember my own father always made me feel like I owed him because he raised me, put food on the table, and bought me clothes. Man, how I hated it when he went on like that."

"Is that why we hardly ever see him?"

"Something like that. He and I just don't see the world the same way. But I want it to be totally different between you and me. This business—I know it's your money that will get it started. So we're gonna do it as a partnership. You will be co-owner. You don't have to work there or anything. But you'll own half of everything. It's called being a silent partner."

I stopped chewing and stared into my mashed potatoes, thinking, now I'm a silent partner, half-owner of a weedy lot that's about to become a used car business on the highway. What was I to say? "Wow."

I always knew my old man could be pushy but I didn't think he'd do this. I hated that I was still being treated like a kid. I wanted to yell at him and tell him what I really felt. But something in me made me stay quiet. I was seething but I didn't feel like I was ready to stand up to him. Not right now, anyway. And maybe, just maybe, this would be a good thing. Maybe he knew what he was doing and it would all turn out okay. Maybe I should just have faith in him.

He looked directly at me now, quite serious. "You're okay with this, right? A father-son thing?"

I was about to say what I was feeling but I stopped. I took a deep breath. "Yeah," I said halfheartedly. "I'm cool with it. What do I do, write you a check, or what?"

"Yep. I'm meeting with the bank in the morning."

"Why the bank?"

"Can't really get this going with just your money. I'll need a loan. Gotta do this right. Gotta spend money to make money."

"So you take my fifty and ..."

"I'm gonna need a little more. Now that I've done the math. If I can put down sixty-five, I can negotiate a better rate from the bank. The bastards'll try to squeeze every penny out of you."

"Sixty-five thousand."

"You're okay with that, right?"

"Sure," I said. "I'm okay with that." But I don't know if I was really okay or not. Everything was so confusing. I swallowed hard. "Dad," I said. "What was Mom really crying about tonight."

He just shook his head. "Well, like I said, I quit my job today."

"Oh," I said, "and she didn't think that was a good idea?"

"Nope."

There was a long pause just then, and he shrugged. "Don't worry. I know how to make her feel better. Ever since we've been married, she's been wanting nicer things than we could afford. Now we can afford them. Now I can make her happy." And he closed the lid on the laptop, walked into the living room, and switched on the TV to the nightly news.

chapter*eleven*

I didn't want to argue with my father on this, but my gut instinct told me he should not have quit his job. That really pissed me off. Maybe this time my mother had a good reason to cry.

I knocked on her bedroom door.

"Go away," she said. I was guessing she thought it was my dad.

"It's me," I said.

I heard her blow her nose. "What is it, Brandon?"

"Can I come in?"

"Sure."

I opened the door and walked in. The room was a bit of a mess and so was my mom. "He shouldn't have quit his job like that," I said. "Not right away."

She shook her head. "There's no changing that now." She didn't look up at me.

"I know," I said. "I feel like this is all my fault."

Now the floodgates opened more and she started crying again. "No, Brandon." The arms were out. I walked toward her. She stood up and hugged me. "No, it isn't your fault. You didn't tell him to quit his job."

"I kinda wish he had discussed all this with me before moving ahead."

She released me and blew her nose. "You know your father." I looked at my mom as she sat back down on the bed and tried to pull herself together. She didn't look too good tonight but I knew that usually she was a really good-looking woman. There was a picture on the dresser of her and my dad when they were, like, twenty-one. They both looked so young, so happy, and she was a knockout. My father had always been ambitious, had talked about making it big. For him, that had always meant money. He worked hard at what he did but, like me, he'd always said he didn't have any luck. We'd both been unlucky bastards. Up until now.

But why all the unhappiness then?

I knew I couldn't own up to the true way I was feeling about my father's stupid decision and the way he was treating me. So I decided to suck it up and try to put a good face on it. "Mom," I said, "this is going to work out. I promise."

"You know your father's tried his hand at owning his own business before."

"Yeah, I remember." My father had once saved $10,000 and bought a truck and equipment for steam cleaning carpets in people's houses. He couldn't make a go of it. And the second time he started a business, it was landscaping. That one went even worse.

"Well," I said, "at least this time he's doing something he understands. Selling cars. Apparently, I own half the business." I tried to make it sound like I thought this was a good thing. But it didn't come out that way.

My mom looked me in the eye. "I'm sorry, Brandon. *You* won the lottery. It's your money, not ours. Not his."

"I'm good with it. I've got lots in the bank. Don't worry about me." I didn't really think I had much of a choice. Besides, it was already done. It was too late. Let my dad do his thing and maybe this time he would have his dream come true.

"He used to buy lottery tickets every week," my mom said.

"I didn't know that."

"He spent fifty dollars each week. And we didn't have it to spare. He kept saying it increased his chances of winning."

"But he never won?"

"He won a few free tickets. Ten dollars here. Twenty there. That's all."

"I guess that's true of most people, right? What are the odds of winning?"

"Ridiculously low."

"But he quit?"

"He gave up the lottery, but then, one night, after we'd had an argument—about money, of course—he emptied our bank account. We only had two thousand dollars but he took it out and went to the casino. He lost it all within two hours."

"What did you do?"

"I nearly left him."

"I wouldn't blame you."

"But I was pregnant with you."

"Oh."

"So you saved the marriage, Brandon."

"No. Sounds like you saved the marriage."

"Well, I stayed with him. He didn't gamble again."

We could both hear my dad's voice now. He was on the phone to someone. All I could tell was that he sounded rather business-like. He was probably working on his "deal"—his new business. It was now becoming a bit clearer that my partner, my dad, was a gambler on a lot of fronts. He had gambled his savings; he had gambled on the possibility of losing my mom. He had cleaned up his act, though, and made his living, paycheck to paycheck. But now he was banking on me and banking on the fact he could make a profit from owning his own car lot. And I was along for the ride. Or I *was* the ride.

"So, I'm going to have to help him make this new business thing work," I said.

"I'm not sure I like that," she said. "You need your own life. You need to figure out what you want to do."

But I had no clue about what I wanted to do. My current plan was to finish school. Or not finish school, if I didn't want to. I mean, why bother? I could live off of what I'd won. If I was smart, and not crazy, I would never have to work a day in my life.

I didn't mention any of this to my mom.

I gave my mom a kiss on the forehead. "I think everything is going to be okay," I told her, and then she stood up and gave me a hug. But I knew that so much was about to change. So much had already changed.

I was thinking about going back downstairs and trying to learn more about the business I was about to get into (or at least bankroll), but my dad was still on the phone and deeply involved in something involving "inventory" and "markup," and I decided to let sleeping dogs lie.

Back on the computer, it was like stepping into my own little fantasy world. My inbox was even more crowded. Old friends had resurfaced to renew their friendship. Even kids I hadn't seen since grade one. I had new friends near and far. I had adults begging me for money to save someone who was sick in their family. Fathers losing their home to the bank, mothers trying to get their sons into rehab and needing cash.

And girls. There were girls from school sending me short little notes asking to get together. And girls near and far who wanted to be my "friend." Some of them sent pictures. Pretty girls with very sexy looks.

I knew I was probably being foolish but I rather liked my own little lotto fantasyland, and it seemed so much more interesting than video games or reality TV shows. This was my life. And I had some seriously hot chicks wanting to be my friends.

So I wrote back to a few of them. What could it hurt?

"Thanks for writing," I'd begin. "You sound like a very interesting person. Tell me a bit more about yourself."

I wasn't much of a writer. But I was curious.

I had to remind myself that they were writing to me not because they wanted to get to know me. (Hey, I'd been me all my life and there had been no girls queuing up in my inbox.) They were interested in the guy who had won the three mill. They were all that shallow.

But it was a game, right? And I'd have some fun playing the game.

In fact, after I'd answered the twelfth e-mail from a beautiful girl who I had never met (I was only answering the ones who'd sent photos), I was thinking that this was more fun than I'd had most of my life. For number thirteen, I just cut and pasted my little now-standardized reply to number twelve into the message and fired that one off.

Back in my inbox, I discovered a message from Taylor. *Brandon, I was hoping you'd call. I sent you a text but you didn't respond. Are you okay?*

I looked down at the faded ink on my hand and then at her cell phone number that I had scrawled on the pad on my desk. I couldn't comprehend that Taylor was actually interested in me. As I pictured her in my head, I could feel my heart beating faster. I almost reached for the phone. But I didn't.

chapter**twelve**

Needless to say, I forgot to do my "homework" for Mr. Carver. He hadn't given me a deadline. In fact, I didn't really see what the point was, but it would have to happen at a later date.

In the morning, my inbox had more of those tantalizing incoming messages, including some from the girls I'd written back to. I was running late but I peeked at one. It was the twenty-one year-old woman, and the photo this time was of her on the beach in the summer in a very skimpy bathing suit. Oh yes. It turned out she—her name was Sheila—lived in a town not far away and she thought that I looked "cute" from the picture she saw of me in the paper. (Well, hell, any guy would probably look cute to her, standing with a check for three million dollars.) She ended her note with: *Maybe I can drive over and pick you up, and we could go out for coffee to get to know each other.*

Oh boy.

I felt a little dizzy again.

Just then my dad yelled up to me that he'd drive me to school. That was new. But then, my dad was now unemployed.

Did I actually want to move from fantasy world to reality and meet this Sheila—who was drop-dead gorgeous but obviously only interested in my wallet and not me? I would have to think about this. And school. Why the hell was I going to school?

My only answer was this: *Right now, I don't know what else to do other than keep doing the things I was doing before I won.* So I figured I would go to school.

As we got into the car, my dad said, "I know you had a talk with your mother. I apologized to her and told her I would be careful. Don't worry—I will make this work. I'm meeting with the landowners today and then the bank. You're still feeling okay about this?"

My dad was a little calmer about his business plans today, less like the salesman (and bully) that he could sometimes be. I felt trapped and uncertain about me and about what was going to happen to my family. I squirmed in my seat but I didn't see any real turning back. "Sure, I'm okay with what we talked about. It's now or never."

He smiled.

I saw Grant Freeman sitting outside on the wall at school with a couple of his buddies from the track team. I thought about going over to him and just saying I was sorry so we could let that shit go. But I didn't. I should have, but I didn't.

I also noticed Kayla near the door but, as soon as she saw me, she turned and walked inside and was swallowed into the crowd. I didn't try to follow her. Kayla was the only one who didn't seem totally thrilled with my luck. What was that all about? I had been friends with Kayla for a long time. We'd shared a hell of a lot together. But climbing trees was definitely a thing of the past for me. And maybe Kayla was, too. That was a hard thought, but I was hanging onto that image of Sheila in my head and there was Taylor as well. Taylor was used to having any guy at her beck and call. I was wondering if the fact I hadn't called her and hadn't answered her text or e-mail was driving her crazy. That thought made me smile.

I had a hard time concentrating in English and history classes. I was realizing again that this was not my final year. Almost everyone there beside me in history was one year younger than me. I sorely regretted having to repeat that one school year so that I was a year behind everyone my age. It was my own fault for being lazy. And now I was stuck here to endure this year and then one more full school year. That seemed like forever. I wanted to get on with my life.

Mrs. Waverley was trying to teach us about the Great Depression of the 1930s. I knew very little about it and it seemed so far back in time, I wondered why it even mattered. It began with a stock market crash in 1929. At the worst point of the Depression, over a quarter of the working population was out of work and couldn't find a job. People lost their homes and farms, and all across North America there were camps of people with no money, no jobs, not enough food, and very little hope. Over fifty percent of the kids were malnourished.

Many schools were closed as millions of kids just stopped going to school. Over 200,000 took to hopping freight trains and moving away, hoping to find a better life somewhere else.

Mrs. Waverley seemed to be rather animated about the whole thing. "Who was to blame for it all? Some say the banks; some say the free market system. Some blamed the government for not doing enough. What do you think?"

Not that any of us really knew enough about it to have an opinion. But it was John Gardner, editor of the school paper, who adjusted his rimless glasses and piped up. "I'll bet it was the rich people. When things got tight, I bet they just looked out for themselves and let everyone else starve." John was always one of the first to have a political opinion about anything. "And the banks," he added. "Look at what happened in 2009. The fat cats were so greedy that they nearly caused a total meltdown of the economy. All they wanted was more profit. When it all went bust—all those bad loans, bad investments—they got bailed out by government. It could happen again anytime."

You could tell Mrs. Waverley liked John and his opinions. "Yes, it probably could happen again. I hope it doesn't. But what would you do if there was another depression?"

The faces looked blank. This was my generation. We'd grown up in a pretty comfortable world. What did most of us know of poverty? In my own head, I was thinking about me and my family, how I could use my money to keep us all going, to protect us. But what if we were the only rich, comfortable family in a world of homeless, starving people?

Or what if something happened to the banks and I actually lost all the money I'd won?

It was starting to sink in how little I understood about money, or banks, or investments, or anything financial, really. All my life, I'd considered myself a person who was not very bright. School had always been a struggle. *Dumb kid* had been a label that stuck with me when I was younger. Was I really stupid? Or was it really just mental laziness on my part?

Maybe I couldn't afford to be dumb or lazy anymore.

John Gardner finally broke the silence again to answer Mrs. Waverley's question. "I'd go live in the woods somewhere and learn how to live off the land." He was dead serious. I watched as my other classmates just laughed at him. But that didn't seem to bother him at all. I was one of the few who wasn't laughing, because I knew that John was one of the smartest kids in school. John's answer wasn't a joke. He meant it. And if he had to, he could probably do just what he said because he was the smart one. So the others were laughing at him because he was smart. I, too, had had kids laugh at me for answers I gave in class. But they had laughed because they thought my answers were lame. They were laughing at *me* because they thought I was dumb. Very weird.

John noticed that I wasn't laughing. He looked right at me as Mrs. Waverley tried to get the class to quiet down. When class was over and I was walking down the hall, John walked up beside me. "Thanks, dude."

"What for?"

"For not laughing."

"You think you could really learn to live off the land?"

John adjusted his glasses. "It wouldn't be easy. But I'd learn. If there was a crash, I'd want to be away from the cities and suburbs. I'd want some control over my own destiny."

"Makes sense."

"Now you," John said, adjusting his glasses, "you'd be like the Rockefellers and Kennedys of the Depression."

"I don't get it."

"Some of the rich actually got richer during the Depression. Same thing happened in 2009. People used other people's misfortune to profit from."

"I wouldn't do that," I said.

"You already did." His voice had a funny edge to it now. And his face had changed. He had a hard look. I should have known. There was not an idea ever put forward in a classroom that John didn't challenge somehow.

"What are you talking about?"

"You gambled and you won. So everyone else lost."

"I'm not really a gambler."

"I know. I read the story. First time, right?"

"It was a freaky thing. Just happened."

"But you became the poster boy for lotteries. You're famous. A kid who buys one lottery ticket and is set for life."

"So?"

"So, now a lot of people out there are saying, if it can happen to him, it can happen to me. So they buy lottery tickets, they gamble; they go online, they gamble. Turns out it's the people who are poor who spend the most money on gambling. It becomes like a disease for some."

"Yeah, but I can't change the way things happened. I'm not out there telling people to gamble."

"Dude, you don't have to. Your story is everywhere. You're like a frigging hero and all you did was plunk down five bucks. You know the suicide rate of pathological gamblers is double that of everyone else?"

"Give me a break," I said. I didn't need this heavy guilt trip. I was now truly wishing I could shake Mr. Smart Ass.

"I didn't do anything wrong."

"Then give it away."

"What?"

"Yeah, give it away. Make the money do good."

"Easy for you to say."

"I'd do it," he said. "Freak them all out. Find a way to do some real good with it and just go for it."

"Not gonna happen," I said. John stopped in his tracks and I was thrilled that I could go on my way without him preaching to me. I walked on but then turned back to look at him. When he saw me turn around, he made a nasty face and then gave me the finger.

chapter*thirteen*

At lunch I saw Kayla, sitting alone in the cafeteria looking rather sullen, so I went over and sat down beside her. She hardly looked up from her sandwich.

"Hey," I said.

"Hey."

"I had a lecture this morning from John Gardner. He says I should give away all my money."

"Maybe you should."

"My dad already has plans for some of it."

"And you?"

"I actually haven't figured out what I want to do with it. But I'm seriously considering quitting school. Just don't think I can handle another year of this."

Kayla just gave me a look that told me she thought I was being stupid.

I looked around at the chaos of the lunchtime cafeteria. "I mean, there must be more to life than this."

"Brando, what is it you want?"

"I don't know, to tell you the truth."

"Then you have to be careful. If you don't know what you want, you need to stick with what you know until you figure it out."

"But I'm getting kind of restless."

"Just don't do anything stupid." There. She said it out loud. Kayla tossed a half-eaten sandwich into the paper bag and got up. "I need to go get a book in the library," she said sullenly. And left.

This was so unlike Kayla. She had never ever treated me like this before. But lately it had been different. Something about her had changed.

Or maybe something about me had changed.

I checked my cell phone for text messages and discovered one from Taylor there. MEET ME BY THE GYM AT 12:30. I looked at my watch. 12:40. What the hell.

I sprinted down the hallway and saw Taylor standing by herself by the outside doors. She turned my way and smiled as she watched me running toward her.

"I didn't think you were coming," she said.

"Just got your message. What's up?"

"I've got my mom's car. Wanna go for a ride?"

"Sure." How could I turn this down?

Taylor's mother's car was a silver BMW. The horn sounded and the lights flashed briefly as she unlocked it from halfway across the parking lot. "You didn't call," she said.

"I had some ... um ... stuff going on," I said sheepishly.

"How's Kayla?" she asked.

"What do you mean?"

"You two always seem to be together."

"We've been friends for a long time."

"Oh, I see."

I got in the car and, as Taylor sat down beside me in the driver's seat, I suddenly felt trapped and nervous. She noticed right away.

"Relax," she said, putting a hand on my leg.

"I am relaxed," I answered. "Where are we going?"

Taylor fired up the engine and snapped her seatbelt on. "The beach," she said.

The ocean was nearly an hour's drive away. I had been thinking she just wanted to drive around the block for a coffee in the time left for lunch hour. "To the beach," I repeated.

Taylor put on a pair of sunglasses as we drove out the driveway of the school and onto the road. And I was thinking this was so unreal. Me cutting classes and heading to the beach with Taylor Reynolds. The girl looked totally sexy in her shades. She cranked up the music loud. It was an old AC/DC tune. The sound system was outrageous. But the tune was all wrong.

When the song ended, she turned the music off.

"You're a metalhead?" I asked.

She tilted the shades down on her nose. "Does that surprise you?"

"Well, yeah."

"I'm not what you think," she said.

"I didn't mean it like that."

"Well, I'm not what everyone would tell you about me."

"In case you haven't noticed," I said, "I don't usually have a lot of people sharing their latest gossip with me personally."

"That's good." She reached in her purse and pulled out a very fat joint. "Want some?"

Another surprise. I wondered if this was some kind of test. I was in totally unfamiliar territory here. I figured I was supposed to say yes, but I was already in the deep end of the pool. I'd been stoned before, for sure. But this didn't seem like the time or place.

"Nah, not really," I answered sheepishly.

"Cool," she said, tucking the joint back into her purse.

I felt I needed to explain. "It's not that ..." I started to say.

Taylor shook her head. "Not to worry. I like you just the way you are."

"You too," I said awkwardly, wondering right away if that made any sense.

Taylor laughed. But it was a sweet laugh. "Brandon, you don't need to do anything you don't want to do. You need to be you."

"I'm just not sure who I am anymore."

"Well, I'm gonna have to help you figure that out. Otherwise, some of those buttheads at school are gonna have their way with you."

"What do you mean?"

"You've already got one enemy. Grant Freeman can be a flaming asshole. I know. He used to be my boyfriend."

"I meant to apologize to him."

"Don't. He'd see that as a sign of weakness. Just watch out if *he* tries to apologize to you and wants to be your friend."

"Why?"

"Grant is Grant. But the ladies—that's a different story. You're never gonna know who's real and who isn't. In case you haven't noticed, you are the subject of much discussion."

"You should see the e-mails I'm getting."

"I can imagine. Did you answer any?"

I might have blushed then. "A few."

"Let me guess. The ones who sent pictures, right?"

"A couple."

Taylor took her sunglasses off and briefly looked away from the road to look me in the eye. "So now you're beginning to know what it feels like to be the center of attention. I've been there most of my life. It ain't always easy. In my case, people judge me for what I look like, not who I am."

"Guess that's been true for me, too. But in my case, it was kind of the opposite of you."

"But now it's different," Taylor continued. "People will want to be your friend. They'll want to be with you. They'll want something *from* you."

"All because of the money, right?" I said, sounding rather dejected.

"Poor little rich boy."

The conversation certainly wasn't going anywhere near where I thought it would go. And Taylor was not the girl I thought she was. "So why did you write your phone number on my hand?"

"Well, because you caught my attention. I thought your problem was interesting."

A minute later when she stopped for a red light, she leaned across and kissed me hard on the mouth and lingered there long enough for the light to change and a driver behind us to honk his horn. When she pulled away, I could hardly breathe.

chapter**fourteen**

The summer crowds had faded and the beach was mostly empty. We took off our shoes and went walking in the sand. I told her the whole story about Kayla and me climbing trees. Even the part about her kissing me and me falling out and what happened after that.

"And now she's mad at you, right?"

"Yeah. And I'm not sure why."

"Because you're changing, Brandon. Your circumstance has changed. Everything about you is going to change. She's missing the old you."

"In some ways, so am I."

"Kayla would be really pissed if she knew you were with me right now."

"How do you know that?"

"Trust me, I know." And of course she was right. "Just don't give up on her. She may get to like the new you."

We sat down on the rocks by a jetty and watched some surfers in the water catching some very clean shoulder-high waves. "I'd like to try that," I said.

"I had a few lessons," Taylor said. "It's not easy at first, but once you get it, it's a total stoke. Hey, maybe you should learn to surf. Put it on your list."

"What list?"

"The list of things you're going to do with your life, now that money has given you the freedom to do whatever you want."

"Is that what I have?" I asked, looking up at a dozen or so seagulls that were swirling round in the blue sky above. "Freedom?"

"You do. As long as you take charge. That's one of the things I learned along the way. You hungry?"

"Actually, I am. I didn't eat lunch."

"Neither did I. Let's go find someplace expensive. You're buying, right?"

I laughed. "So that's how you take charge?"

"That's it."

And an expensive meal it was. It came to over a hundred dollars and I didn't have that much with me. I'd left most of my cash and my credit cards at home. So, in the end, we split the cost. Taylor didn't seem to mind at all. She smiled. "We're going to have to work on you a bit. Bring you up to speed."

On the drive home, she told me the story of her life. Parents divorced when she was young, mom remarried to an asshole. Divorced. Remarried to another asshole. "It's like she's a magnet for them. But now she's single again. And I feel like I never really had a father at all. What about your parents?"

I told her about my mom and about my dad and his current plans.

"You're lucky. You have them both. Be good to them." Almost every time she opened her mouth, she surprised me with what she had to say. She wasn't at all the bitchy, spoiled, hot girl that I had imagined.

Taylor stopped in front of my house. A couple of kids from school were across the street and looked our way. While they were watching, she leaned across and kissed me again. First she put her tongue in my ear and I felt her breasts pushing up against me. Then she took my face in her hands and kissed me like the first time at the stoplight. I thought I'd died and gone to heaven.

When I walked into the house, there was new furniture in the living room and my mom was smiling. "What do you think?" she asked.

The truth was I liked our old furniture. Now the place looked different and it didn't quite seem comfortable any more. I wasn't at all sure I liked the change. But my mom was happy. So what the heck. "It's looks great," I said.

When my dad came home, my mom hugged him and he seemed tired but happy. "It's all coming together," he said. "I should be up and running soon. Brandon, I have another appointment at the bank tomorrow around three. I'll pick you up at school and we can run over. Some papers to sign and that sort of thing. Also, they'll have some ideas about what you should be investing your money in."

Now he was pushing me again, taking charge in a way I didn't like at all. I didn't like him making decisions for me, telling me where to be and when, and what to do with my money. But I didn't say anything.

He tapped me lightly on the shoulder. "Trust me. This stuff is important. No time to lose."

I wasn't very hungry for dinner after the expensive late lunch. My mom watched me just push the food around on my plate. I got up after a bit and went up to my room. I still had the feel of Taylor's lips lingering on my mind. Was that for real or was she just using me like she said the others would? By the time I sat down at my computer and checked my e-mail, I realized I was way overdue for a reality check. More requests from desperate people looking for financial help. More self-introductions from girls and women I did not know. Even a couple of guys wondering if I was gay. One guy said I looked gay in the newspaper photos and that kind of ticked me off. Another long e-mail from the twenty-one-year-old who wondered if I'd like to spend the weekend with her at a cottage up the coast. Whoa.

And then this from Kayla: *I never want to speak to you again.*

Someone saw me getting into Taylor's BMW and driving away from the school and reported it to Kayla. I could see what she was thinking.

I called her cell to explain, but as I started to talk, she had only two words for me. "Fuck off," she said and hung up.

I tried calling back but she didn't answer. Then I found myself going back to my inbox and beginning to read the flattering e-mails from my admirers. More unreality. That's when I noticed the list of names by my computer. Right. Carver's "homework."

So I Googled the first name on the list.

Desmond Williams. *Desmond Williams won eight million in the New Jersey Lottery and his girlfriend sued him for half of what he won. His brother, Vic, hired a hit man to try to kill him in hopes of inheriting the wealth. Desmond had his own share of legal problems and ended up in jail after smashing his car into the front of a bank while driving impaired. Within three years, he was living on his own and bankrupt.*

I blinked at the screen, not sure if this was a joke or not. So I Googled the name again and found the same story on a number of sites. Next up on the list was Molly Reilly. She won $5.2 million in an Ontario lottery and within two years lost all her money betting on horse races and gambling in casinos. "Winning the lottery isn't always what people think it would be," she said. She lost her house once she was bankrupt and ended up living in a trailer. "Once the money was gone, all my friends deserted me," she had told the papers. Poor ole Molly.

I was beginning to get the picture.

Number three: Renata Collins. She won $2.2 million in 1997 in Texas and invested most of it in the stock market. Unfortunately, her hotshot financial advisor had picked the wrong stocks. When her nephew came down with a serious illness (and no health insurance), Renata had to liquidate her losing stocks to help him, costing her over a million dollars in medical bills, and before it was all over, the winnings were gone and so was the meager $30,000 she had previously saved toward her retirement.

Number four. David Nobel won a million in California in 2006, quit his job, divorced his wife, and married a much younger woman. They moved to Hawaii and within less than a year, she was divorcing him and taking half of what he had won. After that, depressed and alone, he gave away what was left of his money randomly to people on the street, until all he had left was enough money for airfare back to California, where he got his old job back as a car mechanic at $20 an hour.

Next up was Boyd Carson who won four million, only to get himself addicted to crystal meth. He murdered his drug dealer and ended up in prison.

In 1999, Sylvia Jackson won a cool $12 million and began to give it all away, bit by bit, to environmental organizations, charities for orphans, research for cancer, and almost anyone who asked or who was in need. Unfortunately, she didn't protect any of it for herself and ended up losing her home and filing for bankruptcy.

Dean Smith was another winner from British Columbia whose $5 million win led to divorce, various lawsuits, and family alienation.

Poor Jim Davis won ten million and was almost immediately kidnapped and held for ransom. He was murdered before the police could find him and the murderer was never found.

And finally, Brad Stermer, at age seventy, won an incredible $21 million in an Arizona lottery. He was more than generous to his family, giving away two million each to his four sons, two daughters, and his seven grandchildren. Sadly, one of the teenaged grandsons used his newfound wealth to get addicted to crack cocaine and died of an overdose. Brad's wife left him and many in his family stopped talking to him. He ended up turning to drink for comfort and watched his life go down the toilet.

I guess I could have kept up my research and looked for more. But I'd come to the end of Mr. Carver's list and didn't want to dig further.

chapter*fifteen*

My head was spinning when I went to bed and I had another night of not being able to sleep. I was a little ticked off at Carver for wanting to rain on my parade. None of that bad stuff would happen to me. I wouldn't let it happen.

But it was starting to sink in. I was going to have to use my head. I'd been coasting most of my life. I had never had to look out for my back. And I also had never tried too hard at anything. Never really put my full brain to work.

And I'd been okay with that.

But maybe it wasn't going to work like that anymore.

Maybe having a pile of money was itself like some kind of job. Maybe even a difficult job that you had to work at.

I had a free period in the morning and dropped by Mr. Carver's office. I owed him that for cutting me some slack.

"How's the life of the rich and famous?" he asked.

"I'm learning the ropes."

"Good. You look up those names?"

"Oh, yeah. Man, those people had some bad luck."

"Maybe it was bad decisions."

"I don't know. It didn't seem that way. Some of those people were trying very hard to do the right thing. Even they got screwed."

"You got a plan for avoiding the pitfalls?"

"No plan. But I'm getting a few theories."

"Like?"

"Like going slow."

"Brilliant. I agree."

"Like using my head."

"I like it even better."

"Trouble is, I'm starting to see how every good thing I might want to do could go wrong. Every smart thing I could do might come back and bite me in the ass. So maybe why not just go with the flow and see what happens?"

"Go with the flow," Carver said sarcastically. "Now there's a plan." And he just stared at me.

I didn't particularly like the way that made me feel. "What would you do with the money?" I tossed back at him.

"I can't answer that. I wouldn't have bought the lottery ticket in the first place."

"What if someone had bought it and given it to you—like a birthday present—and then you won?"

"I would have burned the ticket and told no one that I'd won."

"I don't believe it," I said. He had to be bullshitting me.

He laughed. "Okay. You got me. I don't know what I'd do. Maybe I'd be tempted to take it."

"And you really wouldn't quit your job?"

"Nope. I like my job. I told you that. Anyway, this is not about me. It's about you."

Mr. Carver was back to being a little too cocky. I was feeling devilish. "Suppose I decide to start giving money away to people—anyone I want to. Just for the hell of it?"

"Why do that?"

"Just because I can. Maybe it'll do some good."

"Or harm. You read about Jackson and Stermer. I'm sure there were others."

"What if I wanted to give you $20,000? Just for the hell of it?"

"Why would you do that?"

"'Cause I wanted to. Would you accept it?"

"No. I have principles."

"I'm not sure I believe you."

"Brandon, I can see that, in one way, this whole thing has got your brain engaged. I don't know you really well, but it seems to me like you've been sleepwalking through school the whole time you've been here."

I felt a chill run down my spine because that was so true. That was exactly the way school had felt to me.

"But now you're awake. You are fully aware. You're just a tad confused."

"Yeah, I know that. But maybe it's something in the stars. Maybe I was supposed to win the money. Maybe it's just the beginning of a lucky streak."

"Ain't no such thing as a lucky streak. And forget the stars. What are you doing? Reading the astrology column in the mornings now?"

"No. I just think that maybe I have more good luck coming my way. Like you say, my eyes are open now. I'm—what was it?— 'fully engaged.' All I have to do is recognize what's around me, what's going on, and I'll be the luckiest eighteen-year-old on the face of the earth."

Wow. Now I was giving speeches. Carver was so right that this was a new me. I never talked like this before. I just let the world happen—I let events wash over me. This was different.

"About that luck thing. 'Luck,' someone said, 'is a dividend of sweat. The more you sweat, the luckier you get.'"

"Who said that?"

"Guy named Ray Kroc."

"Never heard of him."

"He was the founder of McDonald's."

"Kind of a funny guy to be quoting."

"I'm not saying the man is my kind of hero. I'm just saying he's probably right." The bell rang in the hall. Carver smiled and looked directly at me. "Better get to class, Brandon. Stay in touch, cowboy. Go as slow as you can with whatever you decide. And thanks for dropping in."

I didn't see Kayla at all that day. Taylor found me, though, at my locker and gave me a big hug and a kiss on the cheek, making enough fuss to ensure that plenty of people saw. But it wasn't quite real. More like something you do in a movie. All show.

Back in history class, as North America was moving through the Depression, I was strangely more interested than usual. All that stuff about banks failing, people losing their money. Me, with my afternoon meeting with my first banker. Maybe I was going to have to get up to speed on this financial thing pretty quickly.

And then math class. Numbers. Calculations. Percentages. Mr. Grimer would put a really large number on the board and I saw that number with a dollar sign in front of it. Six zeros in three million, right? What if I could turn three million into ten million? Then what? My dad had already been hinting at me "investing" some of my money. Such a thing had not really occurred to me. *You have money, you spend it.* That's the way it's been for me all my life.

My dad was there at the end of school, right on time. We drove to the bank. My dad seemed a bit nervous and talkative. "You'll like Len Cranmore," he said.

"Who?"

"Guy at the bank. He's set up the loan. And he's a financial advisor."

I nodded. So I was going to have to look at the sober side of this whole thing, maybe. Loans. Investments. Who knows?

Funny thing—walking into the bank. All I'd ever done was take twenty or forty bucks out of the bank machine or deposited a check or two I'd gotten for Christmas, birthdays, or mowing some-one's lawn. I'd always felt like I'd been treated like a kid whenever I'd walked up to a teller. Like I didn't belong there. And now this.

The receptionist led us immediately into Len Cranmore's office.

"Coffee?" she asked me and my dad.

"No, thanks," we both said at once.

Len was all about business. Clean cut. Suit and tie. Picture of his family in a frame on his desk. He handed me a business card and spoke directly to me instead of my father, which seemed weird. "Brandon, congratulations."

"Thanks."

"Hey, lucky us, that you were one of our customers. Thanks for staying with us."

"No problem."

"Now, it's our job—my job—to help you make the most of your winning."

I could tell he was trying hard to sound sincere. Heck, maybe he was. I just knew that we were here because of me and my luck. Len Cranmore would not have loaned me a hundred bucks to buy a bicycle if I'd walked in here three months ago.

"So, Brandon, your father has explained to me about the busi-ness you two will be starting. I assume you're okay with all this?"

I think I hesitated for just a second. Then I looked at my dad. He was looking straight at me. "Sure," I finally said. What was the point in owning up to any doubts now?

"And the loan?"

I looked at my dad. He'd mentioned the loan but we hadn't

really discussed it, and I didn't exactly know why I was part of it. My dad saw the confusion on my face.

"The loan," he began. "I need more than $60,000 to start the business properly, Brandon."

"Then why didn't you just ask for all the money?" I blurted out. Not that I really wanted to be any deeper into this. I just didn't know why he needed even more money.

"Well," he said. "Because it is your money. You're putting up enough. We borrow the rest from the bank."

"And your investments," Cranmore added as he leaned in my direction, "will act as collateral for the loan."

I didn't understand the word "collateral" but decided not to show off my ignorance.

"I didn't want to use the house for that," my dad added.

I wondered why this hadn't been fully discussed. I was thinking now of those lottery disaster stories now. Some of those winners had borrowed money—despite the fact that they had millions. Why were we borrowing money?

"How much is the loan?" I asked Cranmore instead of my dad.

"A hundred," he said.

"A hundred?"

"Thousand," my dad added, looking at my uncertainty.

Cranmore cleared his throat and looked at me. "You'll have to sign for withdrawal of the sixty and then on the loan for the hundred. And then we're going to talk about how you begin to make money on your money. That's the fun part."

The fun part? I knew I was in way over my head and was pissed at my father for not fully explaining what this was all about. But I had to trust him, right? He was my father. And I didn't want to embarrass him or me—showing off my lack of knowledge. And this was a reputable bank, right? It wasn't like we were borrowing from a loan shark. And I didn't want to use my home as—what was it?—collateral.

"If he ... or we ... can't pay back the loan, then what?" I asked.

"That won't happen, Brandon," my dad said.

"But suppose it did?" I asked Len.

"Then the bank would accept some of your investments to cover it."

"Accept" seemed like the wrong word. But I got the point.

"And we pay the bank interest on what's borrowed?"

"That's correct," Cranmore said. "But because you are one of our preferred clients, we can give you just two points over prime."

Two points over prime? He made it sound like "the bank" was doing us a huge favor.

I felt a little like I did at school so often, when I'd be taking a test in something and I'd read the question and didn't have the slightest clue as to what it was asking. It was like that. I sensed a wave of panic rising up in me and then I looked at my father.

He looked at me, nervous and hopeful. This was his dream. His big break. He'd been talking about "getting lucky" all my life. I couldn't back down now.

"I'm good with all that," I said.

"Great," Cranmore said. "Here's the paperwork for you to sign. You can take it home first and read it if you want."

I turned to my dad, "You've already read all this?"

He sheepishly nodded, yes.

"Then I'm cool." And I signed everything—four copies of each. One for me. One for my dad. Two for the bank. Cranmore seemed pretty happy about everything.

"Now for the fun part," he said.

I was wondering if there would be cake and ice cream.

Nope, just a folder with a bunch of papers—one set for me, one for my dad.

"Right now, your money is sitting in a savings account getting very little interest. We want you to be making much more than that and I've got some ideas."

I flipped through the pages. There were lots of color images of people smiling. All older men and women. No kids smiling, anywhere. No teenagers.

"How much can I make on what I have?" I asked.

"Depends on your level of risk acceptance."

"My what?"

"How much risk can you handle?"

I looked at my father. "We're gonna have to study this a bit," he said.

Cranmore continued. "Rightfully so. See, Brandon, the thing is, you can be safe and make maybe two or three percent interest. Get a little more aggressive and earn six to ten percent a year, or be a bit more daring and maybe make twenty percent or higher."

I guess I should have been paying better attention at math. Twenty percent of a few million dollars would be how much? All on top of what I already owned. Wow.

"But the higher the potential earnings, almost always the more risk, right?" my dad asked.

"Yes. And that's the big one. I'm going to suggest you put some in low risk, some in medium, and some in high. Let's do it in thirds. We're talking money market, bonds, mutual funds, and some stocks—gold, utilities." Clearly Cranmore was excited. This was the "fun" part after all. Playing with other people's money.

"We're going to take this home and walk it through," my dad said, which let me off the hook. I felt good about that.

"Any questions?" Cranmore asked.

"Not right now," I said.

He was all smiles. I started to stand up.

"Oh, sorry," Cranmore said. "I almost forgot. A couple more things for you to sign, Brandon." He slid another page filled with words in tiny print in front of me.

"What's this one?"

He took something small out of his desk and slapped it down in front of me. "A new credit card, with some extra advantages. It's platinum."

I stared at the shiny piece of plastic with the gleaming hologram of a bird on it.

I signed another document that I had not read and picked up the card.

"Sign the back," Cranmore said. "Use this pen. Keep it if you like."

And so I signed my name again. And then stared at the card. I didn't know what platinum meant, but Cranmore had made it sound like it was something pretty important.

"Your limit is seventy," he added. The look on my face said it all. "Seventy thousand. We can raise that any time if you request or approach the limit. We call it an 'Infinite card.' Any time you near the limit, we automatically raise the limit. Infinite, of course, means there is no limit." And he couldn't help but smile and laugh a little.

I held the credit card in my hand. And yeah, I remembered the term "infinite" from math. "No limit? That's a joke, right?" I asked.

"Nope. No joke. Like I said, you are one of our preferred customers." Cranmore handed me another business card. "I'm assigned to you. Whatever your banking needs, you call me. I'll take care of it."

I put the credit card into my cashless wallet.

"Kelly out there will walk you through how to use it in the ATMs. She'll set you up with a PIN and you can use it anywhere, anytime, anyplace."

If I'd walked into Cranmore's office feeling nervous and then confused, I walked out feeling like gravity had ceased to exist. I could buy anything I wanted, take money out of machines. The possibilities were, well, infinite.

chapter*sixteen*

Fast forward to later that month: the new me.

I now knew all about mutual funds, floating interest rates, stolen credit cards. (Yes, mine was stolen and used to buy some strange stuff, before the thief was cut off and my card was replaced.) My wallet went missing one day at school, so I phoned the bank. The bank replaced my stolen credit card almost instantly. They assumed the cost of the goods bought on the card as well. I guess I shouldn't have kept a copy of my PIN in my wallet with the card. I think it was Grant who stole it but I couldn't prove it. No one was ever charged, though. It turned out to be no big deal, and when Len Cranmore handed me my new card, he said they'd raised the spending limit even higher than what it had originally been. What's with that?

With my new credit card in hand, Taylor had given me a make-over. I'd resisted at first but finally gave in. First, there was the haircut and then the clothes. These were not clothes you could climb trees in. These were clothes like you see on people on TV. It was so not me—at first. My mom commented about the changes. She wasn't sure she liked the new look, the new me. And she made it clear that she didn't like Taylor and her influence on me.

But, by that time, I was feeling better about the new me. I started to get used to the attention, the clothes, and the feel of having money and even a kind of respect.

In fact, I was starting to get used to a lot of things that were really different.

I could walk into a store and buy the latest technology for music, videos, Internet—whatever I wanted. Just find something I liked and insert a plastic card. Often Taylor was my guide. She never asked me for anything for herself but I bought her stuff sometimes.

And I better stop here and explain. Taylor was *not* my girlfriend.

"Let's get one thing straight," she said, the third week into our so-called friendship. "I'm not your girlfriend." It was right after that that she squeezed up hard against me in her car and kissed me long and hard on the mouth.

"So, you're not my girlfriend," I said, kissing her back.

"We'll work on finding some dates for you." By *we* she meant her, and I didn't quite get it. "I've been giving this some serious thought." She pulled out a list.

"Alexis is probably too smart for you," she said, crossing her off the list.

"Ouch," I said. "That hurts."

"Brandon, I didn't mean it as an insult. You've never been the sharpest knife in the drawer. You are who you are." She paused. "But you are not who you *were*. You are the new, improved Brandon. Thanks to me. You are fine. Intelligence is not that important. Have you taken a good look at people who are famous or successful? Brains are usually not the reason. Looks count. Image counts. Cool counts. And money."

"So Alexis is no good?"

"No. And Danielle. Not for you. Way too shallow."

"I thought it was all about looks and image and cool. Danielle definitely has all three." Most guys thought Danielle was almost as hot as Taylor.

"Trust me. I've known Danielle for a long time. She chews guys up and spits them out. It's what she does. It's what she's good at."

"But let me get this straight. You are trying to set me up with a girlfriend?"

"Not a single girlfriend. You aren't ready for that. You need girls to date, to go out with. To be seen with."

Suffice it to say I was more than a little confused. I really liked Taylor. "Why don't you be my girlfriend?" I asked.

She took my face in her hand the way she did sometimes, gently pinching my cheeks. "You're cute when you're stupid like this, ya know?"

"Thanks."

"Let me explain. When I heard about you winning, I thought

I would get to know you, see how you react, watch how the money changes you, how it changes everything. Yes, I'd become your friend."

"Because of the money?"

"And the notoriety. You are the closest we have to famous in our school."

"Would you have been my 'friend' otherwise?"

"Probably not. You weren't even on my radar."

"Doesn't that make you shallow?"

She seemed a little hurt. "Brandon, I'm trying to help you. Remember how I explained that you and I are in one way alike? We both get a lot of attention. People talk about us, watch the things we do."

In truth, we were nothing alike. But I decided not to answer. I liked spending time with Taylor. I thought she was a little nuts. But I didn't mind whatever she was doing—trying to help me or whatever.

"Brianna is too immature for you. And Emma ... well, Emma is just Emma."

"Who's left?"

"Chelsea is a possibility. And Leandra. Try a movie or dinner. But if it's a restaurant date, I'm gonna have to coach you about what to order. Leandra's father owns an engineering company. She didn't grow up eating hot dogs."

"Coach?"

"What?"

"You used the word 'coach.' Is that who you are? My coach?"

Taylor smiled then and started to laugh, but cut herself off and grabbed my cheeks and planted that famous kiss on my lips. "You're so cute, you know."

"Anything you say, Coach."

And I did go out on a date with Chelsea. I picked her up in a rented limo with a driver. Taylor had advised against it. She said it would make Chelsea think I was too serious, but I wanted to see what it was like.

I liked it. It was kind of expensive. But I'd been wanting to try it and Chelsea was just the ticket. I wanted to be seen with Chelsea—her tall, sleek body and long dark hair. I had on my new clothes, my new look.

The date was okay but lacking something. Chelsea's mother was a model and Chelsea had often traveled with her to New York, London, L.A., and Paris. Chelsea was used to fancy stuff. She said, "I really like riding in limos. I feel so at home in them. Especially white ones."

My limo was black.

The movie was not that good. I put my arm around her halfway through. But that was about it. I guess you could say there was no chemistry between us.

At home that night in my room, I had to report to Taylor about the evening. Taylor said I shouldn't write off Chelsea. "I already got a text from Leandra and she heard from one of her friends who was at the movies. You were seen arriving with Chelsea in your limo and that is a good thing."

"Why is it a good thing?"

"It generates buzz."

"But Chelsea let me know it was the wrong color limo."

"So next time, you get one the color she likes."

This all sounded so silly. What if one of my dates wanted a pink limo or one with polka dots?

I opened my desk drawer and discovered the bottle of whiskey I had bought a while back. My somewhat disappointing date with Chelsea had left me feeling a little sad and hollow. I cracked the seal on the bottle and took a sip. It burned on the way down. It felt good. I'd tasted this stuff before but it seemed different this time. Sitting in my room alone with the bottle and talking to Taylor on the phone.

"Brandon, are you still there?" Taylor asked.

"Why don't *we* go out on a date?" I said.

"What would be the point?" she asked.

"The point would be because I like you. I like being with you."

"I'll take that as a compliment. Of course you like me."

"We'll do the restaurant thing. This time I'll pay the whole tab. And you can coach me about which fork to use and what to order. And we can be seen together."

"And that might make Chelsea jealous."

"She only went out with me once. And it wasn't so great. Why would she be jealous?"

"'Cause that's the way it works."

I took another quick shot of the whiskey. "And that's good?"

"In a way, yes. More buzz."

The third shot was the one that gave *me* a buzz. I don't know why I was doing this—drinking alone in my room, on the phone to the girl that I wanted to be my girlfriend but who kept reminding me she was not. "So does that mean, yes, you'll do the date?" I asked.

"Oh, hell, why not? Sure."

I put the bottle back into the desk drawer. "Taylor, what if I said it really was you I wanted? Maybe I'm falling in love with you. I don't want those other girls."

"Don't be silly," she said. "I explained all this to you before." She didn't take me seriously at all. I'm not even sure I was taking myself seriously. Maybe it was the whiskey talking. "So when is this big dinner date, Brando?"

This was the first time she called me by my nickname. "Next Friday," I said. "You pick the restaurant and the color of the limo."

"It's gonna cost ya. Won't be cheap."

"I'm okay with that. Should I warn the bank ahead of time?"

"Maybe. And we'll have to make a reservation. *I'll* make the reservation. And I'll drive. No limo. I like driving you places. See ya."

"Bye."

I retrieved the bottle and took another slug. I liked what it was doing to my head.

chapter*seventeen*

My father's car lot had been open for a full week now. He hadn't been home much in the past few weeks. There had been a lot of dinners that were just my mom and me, and leftover meatloaf or spaghetti.

On Saturday, my dad drove my mom and me to his business. We met the two guys he had hired to work there. Kevin and Carew were their names. I wasn't sure I liked either of them. They had that really see-through "I wanna be your best friend" way about them that I'd seen before in car salesmen. Heck, I'd seen my dad put it on a million times. Apparently, it's what you had to do if you wanted to sell cars.

The asphalt was new and very black and the cars were not old clunkers, but recent models all looking waxed and polished.

My dad was leading us around the lot. He waved at some customers looking at SUVs. When we came to a blue Honda Accord, he produced a set of keys and handed them to my mother. "This one's for you," he said.

My mom looked stunned.

"It's got air, satellite radio, GPS. And low mileage. I handpicked it for you."

My mom accepted the keys. I saw the tears well up in her eyes. Then she hugged my dad and I realized I hadn't seen enough of that recently. He seemed really proud of himself, and I was thinking now that this whole business thing was going to be good for him and good for our family.

"Go ahead, take it for a spin," my dad said.

She looked thrilled. "You two come along."

"Not now," my dad said. "I want to talk to Brandon and give you a chance to get to know your new car."

My mom hugged him again and then she hugged me. We were one happy family.

We watched her get in the car, adjust the mirrors, start it up, heard the music from the radio. And then she gingerly drove her new car out into the streets with Kevin and Carew waving to her.

When she was out of sight, my dad asked, "What about you, Brandon? Don't you want a car of your own?"

"I don't have a license yet. You know that."

"But I don't get it. Why don't you sign up for the driver-ed course and get on with it?"

I didn't quite know how to answer that one. I'd thought about it plenty. Sure, I could have my own car, get my license, and drive it anywhere I wanted. On the surface it sounded like the obvious thing for a guy like me to do. It had freedom written all over it. But I hadn't felt motivated to take the first steps. For some reason I'd been holding back. Lack of confidence maybe. I'm not sure.

And I think I knew why.

So many things had changed in my life. Recently, I had made myself grow up so fast. Once I had my license and my car, I knew that I would have made that big step into adulthood. There would be no turning back.

But I had admitted this to no one but myself. I just didn't want to go there yet.

"I guess I'm not quite ready," I told my dad. "Sounds crazy, I know. But there it is."

My dad looked puzzled. Really puzzled.

Just then, the couple looking at the SUV waved to him and he went over to attend to them. Kevin and Carew just seemed to hang back by the mobile building that had been parked there for an office. The two of them seemed to be in a heated discussion about something and not paying attention.

I looked around at all the shiny cars on my dad's lot. I was standing there alone and there was something about the fresh smell of the recently paved asphalt that reminded me of a vacation we had taken as a family when I was a really little kid. Something about that smell made me feel really sad.

Later that day, I had a text message from Chelsea, which rather surprised me. Thanks for the movie. Wanna come over tonight?

I wondered why she was asking. She didn't seem to have had that great of a time. Neither had I. But, if Taylor was right, our date had generated buzz. Maybe Chelsea liked that fact. But I'm not sure I did.

I didn't text back.

I started poking through my e-mails. As usual, I had more than I was willing to read. Pretty soon it would be time to just delete them all, get a new e-mail address and tell almost no one. But I couldn't help but realize it had been a long time since I'd heard from Kayla.

A couple of shots of whiskey later, I discovered this e-mail:

Hi Brandon,

I'm attaching a photo of my dog, Larkin. Larkin is twelve years old and so am I. The vet says that Larkin needs an operation because of cancer and if he doesn't get it he will die. My mom and dad say we can't afford it and that Larkin is an old dog and we should have him put to sleep.

I know you don't know me but I saw you on TV a while back. And I found your e-mail address so I'm writing. I think they said it would cost about $3,000. The vet says that he's sorry that it's so expensive.

I guess you can figure out that I'm writing to you to ask for the money. Sorry about that. I'm really sorry. I just thought I'd try. Attached is a picture of Larkin.

Sincerely,

Martin Blake

Martin included his phone number and his address. And a

photo of Larkin, a rather healthy-looking collie.

I'd read plenty of e-mails and letters requesting money but this one hit me like a ton of bricks. A kid and his dog. How did I know it wasn't a scam? I was about to just ignore it when I changed my mind. Thinking about that kid and his dog really got to me. I dialed the number and a kid answered.

"Martin?"

"Yeah"

"It's Brandon."

"You're kidding."

"No. How's Larkin?"

"About the same."

"If I send you the money, you'll explain it all to your parents and they'll have the operation."

"Yeah, I think so."

"I'm gonna mail you a check, okay?"

"Really?"

"Really. Just don't let your parents tell a lot of people. Just get the operation for Larkin and make sure he gets better."

"Okay."

"Take it easy, dude."

"Thanks. Thanks so much."

And that was my good deed for the day. I wrote a check and put it in an envelope to be mailed in the morning. I felt good about it.

For about ten minutes.

Then I started looking at the other requests that had come in. Mostly people looking for money to get someone in their family or themselves out of some kind of a mess. Some of them I think were bullshit. Some were stupid. And some were just plain sad and real. What if I started writing more checks? What if I decided I could help out at least some of them? How would I pick which ones to help?

And once I got started, wouldn't there be more and more? I'd be playing God. Help this one. Let that one suffer.

I kept scrolling through my e-mails but then noticed I had a new text message on my phone. I'd kept my new cell phone number pretty restricted. It wasn't who I expected. It wasn't Taylor. It was Kayla. I'd sent her my new number a long while back but hadn't heard from her at all.

BRANDON. CALL ME.

I called.

"I'm sorry to bother you," Kayla said. "I'm just feeling really alone and I didn't know who to call."

"What can I do to help?" I asked. The truth was that it was great to hear from Kayla again. I'd missed her.

"I don't know. Be my friend again, I guess."

I was confused when she said this. But she sounded pretty unhappy. She sounded rather lifeless and that wasn't like her at all. I was suddenly feeling really good that she was asking for my help. "Yeah, I can do that."

"Are you busy?"

"Now?"

"Yeah."

"Not really."

"Meet me at the coffee shop down the street from you?"

It was still early. I'd pretend I hadn't read Chelsea's message. She wasn't going to hear from me. But this was Kayla and we had a long history. "Sure," I said. "I'll meet you there."

chapter*eighteen*

Jo's was crowded with kids from school. I was getting used to people looking at me when I walked in anywhere. At first it had felt funny, but now I was used to it. Now I was cool about it.

I saw Kayla sitting at a tiny round table in the back, two cups of coffee on the table. I walked straight toward her, passing by Alexis and a couple of other girls trying to get eye contact with me.

"I'm buying," Kayla said as I sat down. "That one's yours."

"Thanks," I said. I took a sip. It wasn't coffee. It was hot chocolate.

Kayla looked awful. She'd been crying. But I wasn't going to say anything about that.

"Bring back any memories?" she asked, nodding at the cup.

I had to think for a minute. Then I closed my eyes and nodded.

A smile slipped out of me. "Winter," I said. "Your kitchen. After sledding on the big hill."

"After we'd gone down together on your sled, then kept going out onto the pond."

"And went through the ice."

"Good thing the water wasn't deep."

I remembered it now like it was yesterday. "But it was bloody cold walking back to your place. Our clothes froze. My pants were like boards. I almost couldn't walk but you told me to keep moving."

"I had to hold onto your arm and pull you. You could be so stubborn sometimes. And so ready to give up."

I sipped some more hot chocolate and gave her a quirky look. "Me? Never." That got a smile out of her at least. I studied her and watched as the smile faded and something else took over.

"What is it?"

"Sometimes I just feel so alone in the world."

"I think I've felt that way, too."

"But not like what I feel."

I shook my head. I could see from the look of fear in her eyes that this was something much worse than what I had ever felt.

She sipped her hot chocolate and looked around the room in a paranoid way. "But what I feel can get pretty serious. I just want to stay in my room and not leave. Sometimes it lasts for days. I never told you. I always kept it hidden."

It was starting to sink in.

"It's like everything out there in the world scares me. It's a lonely, isolated place I go to, and sometimes have a hard time finding my way back. Especially now."

"Why now?"

"Because I don't have you to pull me back up."

"But I don't remember ever really doing anything to help."

"But you were there."

I started to say something almost cruel. I was going to say that she was the one who had turned against me. She was the one who got mad because I had new friends. Instead, I sat there feeling stunned.

"Most people who have never felt this way don't understand."

"I think I've been there before. I used to want to hide from a lot of things."

"Not like this. All I want to do is sleep. I don't want to get up in the morning. Nothing seems worth doing. I stay in bed and sleep. Nothing else seems to help. If I do get out of the house or go to school, I feel anxious and I still feel like I'm all alone in the world."

"But you were never like this when we hung out together." I was finally starting to see how bad things must be for her. And how little I understood who she really was.

"Sometimes I'd hide it. But usually if I was feeling crappy, you made me feel better. Remember all those times, though, that I said I was sick? Sometimes that was me just hiding from the world."

"And now?"

"Now it's bad. And I don't know how to snap me out of it."

Out of the corner of my eye, I could see someone was walking toward us. It was Alexis, the girl Taylor thought was too smart for me.

"Hi, Brandon," she said to me.

"Hi."

"I like that shirt," Alexis said.

"Thanks." I forgot I had on the clothes Taylor had picked out for me. My new look. Brandon, the cool one, the fashion guy. Brandon, the millionaire playboy.

"You two want to join us?" Alexis nodded to the table where she'd been sitting with a couple of other girls.

I looked at Kayla. She looked downright scared and like she was about to cry.

"Not right now," I said. "But thanks for asking."

"Cool," Alexis said. "See you in school."

"Come on," I said to Kayla. "Let's get out of here."

As we left, I hate to admit it, but I knew what those girls at the table were thinking. *What is he doing with her?*

Kayla seemed to be a little less uptight as we walked around town, the streetlights shining down through the leaves of the trees.

"What can I do to help?" I asked.

"I'm not sure you can. The old Brandon needed me as a friend. The new one doesn't. I guess I needed to be needed."

"I'm still the old Brandon," I said.

"No, you're not. You've been taken over by your girlfriend, Taylor."

"She's not my girlfriend," I said. "But she is my friend."

"You think she'd be your friend if you didn't have money?"

I didn't have to answer that. "Let's not talk about me. Let's talk about you. Maybe you need to see a counselor or something. I could pay for it."

"I've seen a shrink a few times. It hasn't helped. He wanted to put me on medication and I read about the side effects. I don't want to do that."

"What can I do then? Just let me know."

"I have an idea. Follow me."

So I followed her and we walked in silence down the sidewalks until we came to the park. We walked out onto the dewy wet grass until we came to a place that was very familiar, even on this dark night.

"I don't know about this," I said.

"We won't go very high, I promise."

She knew I was nervous about climbing up into a tree after my fall. But I followed her lead as she climbed up from branch to branch of a big old oak tree. She sat down on a really sturdy limb and I sat down beside her. "I feel better now," she said. And we sat in silence as a very full moon rose in the sky before us and I put my arm around her and gave her a hug.

Kayla seemed much better when I walked her home. "Sorry about being mean to you before," she said.

"It's okay."

"And you don't have to hang out with me at school. Just be there for me once in a while."

"But I'll hang out with you. Like before."

"No. Taylor will be there. And some of those friends of hers like Alexis. And Chelsea. I couldn't take that." Oh, yeah. Chelsea.

Alexis would tell Chelsea that she saw me at Jo's with Kayla after I didn't take Chelsea up on her invitation. That would go over well.

"They're not that bad."

"I just couldn't be part of that crowd. I'll be fine."

Before I said goodbye, I told her about Martin and about his dog, Larkin.

"That's sad," she said. "But good. Good that you offered to help. I'm just not sure you can fix everything with money, though."

As I walked home, I realized she was talking about herself. How had I missed the fact that Kayla was so fragile? How could I be so clueless? But what was I supposed to do? Ditch Taylor? No way. I liked having cute girls make a fuss over me.

At home, I took a couple of sips from my bottle and checked out a whack of e-mails in my inbox. If one looked like it was from a girl and if there was a photo attached, I opened it. If I really liked what I saw, I sometimes answered. It was like some kind of weird game, communicating with beautiful young women who I didn't know. But I liked being the center of attention. And I liked that I could have a date with any one of them if I decided to. How lucky could you get?

chapter*nineteen*

"Chelsea's mad at you," Taylor said, greeting me like she was my bodyguard as I got off the bus. "And John Gardner has an editorial in the school paper about greed, gambling, and—you guessed it—you."

"Wow." I said. "I have enemies. What about Grant Freeman?"

"No. Grant wants to be your friend now. He told me." It was just like Taylor to be on top of whatever was going on at school, whether it was her business or not. "I'd steer clear of him, though. Just be polite. He's probably just trying to use you."

"Use me for what?"

"Social climbing?"

"What?"

"Well, the high school version of social climbing. How was your date with Kayla?"

"It wasn't a date."

"You could do much better than her, you know."

"Better? As in my own social climbing?" Even saying that term seemed very odd. From tree climbing to social climbing. I wondered which was more dangerous. And I wondered what right she had to be saying this. I wasn't about to let anyone tell me who I could be seen with. I was about to say that to her but she cut me off.

"You should do something that will blow everyone's mind," Taylor said. "Something audacious."

"You'll have to tell me what audacious means."

"Cheeky. Outrageous. Expensive." Taylor took my arm and walked me inside the school. Yes, as everyone watched.

"Why?" I asked.

"Just so people will talk."

"They're already talking. They notice I look different—thanks to you. Act different."

"But you need to take it up a notch."

"I could arrive at school in a limo. A black limo."

"Good start. But it should be more creative than that. The limo thing has been done."

"I'll work on it."

"Me, too. You're making my last year in high school so much more interesting."

Which, of course, reminded me that it wasn't my last year in high school. Having failed a year, I had one more to go.

Later in the day, during the history test, my mood started to darken as I realized I had not done the readings and I'd paid little attention in class and, at the end of the hour, I was handing in a blank piece of paper. Another F that would not look good. In the past, I had occasionally struggled and earned Ds and been given gifts of a C or higher by some teachers. But lately, I had lost all interest in schoolwork.

Mr. Poirier must have taken a look at my test soon after I handed it in because, before the day was over, I was being summoned back to Mr. Carver's office. He was not a happy camper.

"Brandon," he said, holding up the history test with my name on it. "What is this?"

"A test," I said.

"Your test. Where are the answers?"

I shrugged.

"I took the liberty to check in with your other teachers."

"And?"

"Ds and Fs. This does not look good."

"I guess I've been distracted."

"To that I would add preoccupied, bemused, negligent, indifferent, lackadaisical, cavalier, derelict, slothful, and careless."

"That's a long list."

"Boy wins three million dollars. Boy stops doing schoolwork. Boy flunks out of school."

"Is that what's going to happen?"

"If you don't get straightened out."

"But I don't think I really need school."

"You've said this before. And I don't know much about rich people, but it seems to me there are two kinds. Smart rich people and stupid rich people. No, let me not be so crass. There are actively intelligent rich people and intellectually challenged rich people."

"Seems to me that people are either born with brains or they aren't. I was never one of those kids with much in the way of brains."

"It's not just what you're born with. It's how you use your brain. Now, you could use yours—or at least part of it—to do your schoolwork. I know that doesn't sound all that exciting, compared to life in the fast lane. But it will pay off. The smart rich people hang onto their money and even make more. But the ones who don't use their brain tend to lose the money—or, worse yet, it gets them into trouble."

"Listen, Mr. Carver, I know you're trying to help, but I'm seriously thinking of quitting school," I blurted out.

Carver's eyes widened. He looked not only shocked but angry. "That is the stupidest thing I've heard you say yet."

"Why should it matter to you?"

"It matters. I don't like to see talent wasted."

"What talent?"

"Everyone has talent. I don't know what yours is, but it's there, waiting to be developed."

"Look," I said, "I've had one good bit of luck in my life. And I'm going to capitalize on it."

"Big word. Capitalize."

It was a word my father often used. "I know what you've

been trying to say to me about luck and lotteries and all that money-is-the-root-of-all-evil routine. But those are your opinions, not mine."

He looked like he was about to jump across the desk and grab me by the throat. I was almost scared but I was also getting angry. I felt my heart pounding and I was breathing hard. I felt like he was pushing me hard and I didn't like it. He let out a sigh. "Go back to class," he said, sounding defeated. "Or don't go back to class, if you choose. Just think about it, please. Use your brain."

My meeting with Carver kept bugging me for the rest of the day. At noon I ate lunch with Kayla. I didn't care what the other kids would say about that. She seemed to be doing much better today. I told her about my meeting with the VP. Kayla told me not to even consider dropping out of school.

Later on, during my free period, when Taylor latched onto me again, she said she had an idea. After class we walked to a nearby convenience store and she pointed at the sign for "Lotto Max." Lotto Max tickets cost $10 but the jackpot was $25 million dollars. Leave it to Taylor to come up with an idea like this. I plunked down $10. Then I plunked down a second $10.

As we walked out the door, I gave one ticket to Taylor and she seemed thrilled. That one had been my idea.

The other ticket I carried back to the school. Mr. Carver was still in his office. I knocked and entered. Taylor was with me as I walked in. I set the Lotto Max ticket down on some papers on the desk in front of Mr. Carver. "It's yours," I said. "No strings attached."

Mr. Carver blinked at first. Then his gaze turned to a frown. He looked me directly in the eye.

And then he did a strange thing.

He stood up, picked up the ticket, tore it into tiny bits of paper and threw them at me.

And then he sat back down and looked at the papers in front of him.

Taylor tugged me hard and led me back out the door.

chapter*twenty*

When Kayla saw me walk out of the school with Taylor she gave me a sad little half-smile and walked away. I felt a little guilty, but as Taylor held my arm and tugged me toward her car, it was hard to feel too bad about anything. She put on her sexy sunglasses, and then opened the glove compartment and handed me another pair of very expensive-looking shades. "A little present for you," she said.

I put on the sunglasses and rolled down the window. We drove away from the school with the music from the satellite station blasting. Suffice it to say, we did not drive away unnoticed.

"The trick to being cool," Taylor advised me, "is to pretend that you don't care about anything."

"Why?" I asked.

"Well, I don't really know. You just have to look like you're not trying too hard and you don't care what anyone else thinks of you."

"Like this?" I asked. And I just sat there with my arm out the window and the wind ruffling my hair and my dark OP shades on, looking straight ahead like a zombie.

"That's it. You've got it."

"Got what?" I countered.

"It. You've mastered cool."

So I was officially cool. Doing nothing was cool. Not caring was cool. Not trying was cool. I wanted to laugh out loud but I knew that would not be cool. So I did nothing. And tilted my head sideways and slightly lowered the sunglasses to look at three girls from school standing on the corner. I did this slowly and nonchalantly.

And I could tell from the way they looked at me that this was very, very cool.

And I wanted to say out loud, *How stupid is this?* But instead, I hitched the shades back over my eyes, leaned back in the seat, and listened to the music. Clearly, I had mastered the skill.

My mom was sitting at the kitchen table when I got home. I had not invited Taylor into my house. I didn't have any plans for that. It just didn't seem to make sense. Taylor's world was nothing like my world at home. I'd keep the two separate. I knew my mom didn't like me hanging out with Taylor, and I was afraid if I ever invited Taylor in, the two of them would definitely not hit it off.

My mom was looking at a real estate magazine. She looked up when I walked in.

"How was school, Brandon?"

"Good," I said.

"What did you do today?"

"Nothing." The classic universal response to the school question. "What about you?"

"I'm looking at houses," she said, unusually cheerful and upbeat. She held up the magazine for me to look at a picture of one.

"Big," I said. "Wow."

"Your father thinks we should move."

This hit me like a ton of bricks. "Move?"

"You know how long I've wanted to move out of this old place."

Old place? This was my home. I looked closer at the house listing and saw the price. It was expensive. And then I noticed the location. "You want us to move out of Greenville?" I asked.

"It's only twenty minutes away. And look at how beautiful this house is." My mom was positively beaming. I can't say I'd seen her like that often.

I looked at the house again. Big lawn, two-car garage. "And it's got a swimming pool in the back," she said.

"But I don't want to move," I said, with a bit of an edge to my voice.

She looked up at me like I'd just told her I was Martian. "Why not?"

I didn't really have an answer. But I knew I didn't want to move even twenty minutes away. And I liked our home. This is where I'd grown up. And if I moved, everyone I knew would be back here, twenty minutes away. Taylor. Kayla.

My mom looked confused. I'd popped the bubble. I didn't know what else to say so I just went to my room. As soon as I'd shut the door, though, I felt my head filling up with worries. Kayla. I was still worried about her. And school. What was I going to do about school? What if I got left back again? I deserved it but I couldn't handle yet another year of high school with everyone knowing how stupid I was. And what was I really doing, hanging out with girls like Chelsea and Taylor? What was I thinking?

I realized I had the sunglasses in my shirt pocket and I looked at them. One minute I was the cool one, but now I was just a silly dumb kid alone in his room who didn't have a clue. Who was I kidding?

I made the mistake then of checking my e-mails. More "fan" letters from people I'd never met. A couple from kids at school, but the one that caught my full attention was from Martin. I clicked on it.

Brandon, just writing to say thanks so much for the help. Larkin had the operation and it looked like things would be okay. But when the vet started the operation he realized that things were worse than he expected. Larkin had to be put down. We're all pretty sad. But I feel a little better, knowing someone out there cared. Thanks again.

Your friend,

Martin.

Something about the dog's dying really sealed the whole package for me. I felt like calling Kayla for a shoulder to cry on. But I didn't. Instead, I opened my desk drawer and took a long sip from the bottle I had kept hidden there. I felt the heat as it went down and soon the mild buzz in my head. I took a second slug and then realized the bottle was empty. I tossed it back into the drawer and made a mental note to replenish my supply of refreshments. What could it hurt?

I lay down on my bed and felt more confused than ever. Despite my good luck, I felt uncertain, unsettled. I was a failure at school and I didn't see any way I could buy my way out of that. No way could I handle two more full years of high school after this one; I'd been a poor student right since the start—especially lately. I didn't think I could catch up even if I tried. I'd been read the riot act by Carver. I didn't think I had a chance of catching up. Another major setback at school would really suck.

I must have fallen asleep then, just lying on my bed with my clothes on, but something eventually woke me up and I saw it was eleven o'clock. I had an awful lingering taste in my mouth. The booze. I got up and brushed my teeth, and it was then I heard some noises from downstairs in the kitchen. I decided to go down and see what was up.

The lights were on. It was my dad. He was bent over, looking for something in the refrigerator. It looked like he had just arrived home.

"Hey, Dad," I said. "Man, are you working late." I really hadn't seen much of my father in recent days. He was out of the house before I got up and most days I was in bed before he came home.

He turned around and smiled. "Hey, Brandon. You know if your mother left me any leftovers?"

"I'm sure she did," I said. "She always does."

He looked inside the fridge again and then saw the container he was looking for. He grabbed it and put it into the microwave and clicked it on. "Long day," he said.

"How's it going? The business?"

He sat down at the table and I sat down across from him. He put his hands up in the air. "Good days and not so good days. Ups and downs. You'll have to come by again and visit."

"How about tomorrow?"

"What about school?"

"I need to take a day off."

"Can you afford to do that?"

I shrugged. "Not really, but ..."

"But what?"

"Truth is, school is not going so great."

This caught him off guard. He seemed about to say something critical but stopped himself. "You mention this to your mother?"

"No."

"She'd be pretty upset."

"You don't seem that upset," I said.

"Well, I dropped out of high school, remember?"

"I know. And you're doing okay, right? So who needs it? A lot of what they teach there is stuff you're never going to use in real life, right?"

"How are your grades? Any better than your last report card? That was a bit of a disaster. I thought you were turning things around."

The bell on the microwave rang and my dad pulled the ceramic container out bare-handed, then dropped it on the table and waved his hands in the air. "Damn." He grabbed a fork from a drawer and popped the cover on the food. Steam rose up in front of him.

"Nah. Things are worse. It's my fault. I've been distracted."

"You've always been distracted." My father started to eat and I realized it was rather odd that he didn't seem freaked out by what I was telling him. His son was flunking out of school and he was more interested in shoveling down the pork chop and potatoes my mom had cooked. "So what now?" he said between bites.

"I'm thinking of quitting."

He didn't look up at me but down at the steaming food. "Wow." Then he continued to chew.

There was a moment of silence, and then he said, "Your mother would be *really* upset about that."

"I know. But I'm kinda mad at her right now."

"Why?"

"She's talking about moving."

"Yeah. We've both been talking about moving. Newer house, nicer neighborhood. Possibly a pool in the backyard. Big garage. About time to unload this shit-hole."

I couldn't believe my father was calling our home a "shit-hole."

"I don't want to move."

"But you're talking about quitting school. So why would it matter if we moved to a new neighborhood a few miles down the road?"

"She was looking at places in another town."

"Well, it's not like we'd be moving to a foreign country."

"You don't understand." But then, hell, I didn't understand. Why not move? Why not start over? Heck, if I wanted to, I could move out on my own. Get my own apartment or buy my own house.

"Your mom and I had always dreamed about moving up in the world. Now that I have the business, and access to capital for a down payment, why not? It's finally our time."

What was with this "access to capital" bullshit? Once again he was talking about using something that was really and truly mine, not his. But I couldn't bring myself to ask how much of my money would factor into this new house that I didn't want in a new town that I did not want to live in.

"Maybe we all need a change, Brandon. Maybe you *should* quit school and work with me. Lord knows, I could use the help, and I'm sure you'd do a better job than those two slackers I hired."

That caught me totally off guard. My father was saying it was okay for me to quit school. He was giving me his permission. But I hadn't thought about working for him. Or working for anyone. If I played my cards right, I'd never have to work a day in my life. There was so much I wanted to say right then but I knew it would all come out wrong. Suddenly, I felt very tired and very defeated. "I'm gonna go to bed," I said.

"Sure thing. I'll be off early in the morning, but if you don't go to school tomorrow and you want to come by, you know where to find me."

"Good night."

I fell asleep quickly but woke again an hour later when I heard the arguing. My dad had told my mom about me wanting to quit school. He was obviously all in favor of it and she was not. I knew what her thinking would be. Move into a new town, go to a new school, and everything would work out.

But that wasn't going to happen.

The arguing got louder and then died down. Then I heard my mom crying. I pulled my pillow over my head and tried to get back to sleep.

chapter**twentyone**

When my mom tried to wake me in the morning, I said I wasn't feeling well and didn't want to go to school.

"Don't quit school, Brandon," she said. "We can work something out."

But I didn't even want to think about school. There was no "we" involved. The school was my doing. And I was pretty sure whatever school had to offer me wasn't worth it. But I didn't want to get into a big discussion about it.

"I heard you guys arguing last night," I said. "I'm sorry. It was my fault."

"We argue sometimes. It's a bit more difficult now that he's working such long hours. He and I don't really ever have much of a chance to talk or relate to each other. He says that will change.

But I know your father. He's got what he always wanted."

I got up and let her make me a big breakfast. But I didn't go to school. "I'm glad your father has what he dreamed of. You made that happen for him. He's very grateful, even if he doesn't say it out loud to you."

"I know," I said.

"And now maybe I'll get my dream. If everything works out."

She was talking about moving into a new house. I didn't want to get into that, either.

I ate my breakfast like a good son and kept my mouth shut about my feelings concerning moving. I couldn't handle my mom crying, and if I said what I really felt, she'd be crying for sure.

"I'm going to go see Dad," I said. "I want him to show me around some more."

My mom looked at me with concern. "Just don't make any big decisions. It's just one day off from school. Maybe everything will look different by tomorrow. You want a ride there?"

"No," I said. "I think I'd like to walk."

On my street, men were cutting down three more of the big trees and that didn't seem right. Trees had as much right to be here as people and power lines. It really ticked me off. But I kept walking. It seemed that most of my life I'd been making decisions based on trying to keep everyone around me happy. My parents, my teachers, sometimes my friends. But my so-called new friends had a way of wandering away and not being my friends anymore. The truth is that I think most of them just found me rather boring after a while. Kayla was the only one who hung around. And she was weird. She also had her own set of problems. Maybe we'd stayed friends only because we were a couple of losers.

I didn't mind the walk. My head was starting to clear. When I arrived at my father's business, I saw a big truck with a hoist, lifting a very fancy sign into place. There it was: *DeWolfe's Quality Used Cars—Best Deals in Town Guaranteed.* My dad's dream come true. Leave it to him to go for a monster colorful sign.

He was standing by the workmen as the sign was being bolted onto the tall metal posts. When he saw me, he smiled. "What do you think?"

"I think it rocks," I said.

He beamed and said, "Let's go to my office." His arm was around me. That was rare.

Inside, he shuttled Kevin and Carew back out to "watch the lot." I sat down in front of him, at a rather large, expensive-looking oak desk. "No school today?"

"I took the day off," I said.

"Your mother okay about that?"

"She's okay."

"I've never seen her so excited about anything as the possibility of moving to a new house. She's been talking about that ever since we were married. That why you're here?"

"No," I said. A plan was forming in my head. It wasn't much of a plan but one thing was beginning to be clear to me. I wasn't going to be moving into a new house in a new town with my parents. Maybe they could move and I'd stay in our old house. If I wanted to, I could buy it from them. But I didn't want to totally piss them off. I needed my father on my side.

"I want to work here with you. Like you suggested. At least for a while. See what it's like."

My father never looked happier. And he was a man who had spent most of his adult life dissatisfied and unhappy with one thing or another. He didn't say a word. Instead he handed me a business card. It had my name on it. *Brandon DeWolfe—DeWolfe's Quality Used Cars.*

"I took the liberty of doing them up. Just in case."

I looked at the card and had to admit to myself that it looked very cool. The picture of the car lot. My name. But what really was I getting myself into? "Maybe I'll be no good at it," I said. "Then what?"

"You'll be great. Better than Carew and Kevin. I'm letting Carew go. He just doesn't have what it takes."

"What does it take?"

"It takes the skill to let the customer sell themselves on the car. First, you get to know them. You ask a few questions. Make it personal. Make them feel you are a friend trying to help them out."

Yeah, that was my dad. Always telling me about how to sell myself or how to sell anything. "How about I watch you today and see how you do it?"

"I can't think of anything that would please me more." He looked over my shoulder and outside. "And today's the big day—now the sign is up. Isn't it a beauty?"

"How much did it cost?"

"Gotta spend money to make money," he answered.

I'll cut to the chase and just say it was not at all bad. My dad sold a Toyota to a man who had been by a couple of times before. It was mostly signing paperwork and it all looked a lot like school, but I guess it got the job done. The man seemed happy to get the car at a price he liked. My dad acted like the two of them were old buddies, but when he left, he admitted to me, "Truth is, I hardly made a cent on that sale. But sometimes you have to keep the inventory moving. It's all about momentum."

Kevin talked to a couple of casual car shoppers who arrived on foot. "Never a good sign," my dad said. In the end, they also walked away. Next, Carew was a bit too aggressive with a pretty young woman who arrived in a blue Honda looking for something for off-road driving. She was steered toward a green Subaru Outback wagon. You could tell Carew was a bit too pushy and she didn't last long on the lot.

When a rather paunchy guy in an old Cadillac rolled up to the office during noon hour, while Kevin and Carew were on lunch, my dad said, "Come on, watch the old master at work."

When my dad saw the golf clubs in the back seat of the Caddie, he launched into a spiel about golf courses and golf. I never knew him to have played the game in his life but he sounded like an expert. Pretty soon, Herman, the Caddie driver, was telling a golf story that lost me within thirty seconds.

But my dad seemed enthralled. I just hovered in the background and started to wonder what Taylor was doing in school today. So

I checked my phone and saw I had two messages. One from Taylor, one from Kayla, both asking me where I was. I decided to answer neither. Instead, I followed my dad and Herman to the black Escalade with the tinted windows at the front of the lot. My dad already had the keys with him. He had "read" Herman, even before the man had gotten out of his car. Within minutes, Herman was in the driver's seat and my father was climbing in beside him. You'd think they were a couple of old buddies, heading off for a vacation.

The window rolled down on my dad's side and he leaned out and shouted to me, "Brandon, keep an eye on things until we get back."

It was a funny feeling. Both scary but somehow very cool. *I was in charge of the business*—for right now, at least. Kevin and Carew were gone. My dad was gone. I retreated to the office and sat down at my father's desk. I studied the business card with my name on it and then saw a whole box of them on the table.

I knew that I had enough money that I didn't really have to work at all. The trouble is, I knew I had to do something. Maybe this would be ... fun. Well, maybe it would be interesting, at least. Hell of a lot better than school. And I didn't mind the idea of helping my father. He could be a pain in the ass—all opinions and sometimes bossy—but he was my father.

The phone rang and I answered. Someone looking for a late-model Toyota. I didn't have a clue but suggested the caller come have a look. Oops. Wrong thing to say. He hung up without saying goodbye. Okay, another lesson learned. "Always give the customer what they want," I remembered Dad saying, "even if you don't have it."

I decided not to tell my father about the phone call.

And then a very rusty-looking old Chevy Malibu pulled in and a woman of about thirty got out. I walked out and greeted her.

"Hey," I said. "Can I help you?"

She smiled a kind of sad, desperate smile. "Yeah," she said. "Not much life left in the old beast here," she said pointing at her car. "I need something to replace it but I don't have much money. So I'm looking for something basic but reliable. Do you think you can help?"

"Sure," I said. "Let's look around."

"Oh, thanks," she said. "If I don't have a car, I'll lose my job. If you could help me find something, that would be fabulous."

"I'm Brandon, by the way."

"I'm Faye. Nice to meet you."

So we started walking toward the back of the lot where the cheaper cars were. I really didn't know what was there in the way of expensive or inexpensive cars, but she seemed happy to be following me. She seemed to believe I knew what I was doing. "What kind of work do you do?" I asked.

"I'm a waitress. Work late nights sometimes. Can't have a car breaking down on me late at night or making me late for work."

"I know the feeling," I said. This from a guy who didn't have a driver's license.

"What about this one?" she asked. She was looking at an older Ford Focus with a dent in the car door and a not-so-great-looking paint job. The price was on the info sheet in the window with the year and the mileage. So I just read it off to her and she seemed pleased. "Can I drive it?" she asked.

"Sure," I said. I tried the door. It was open. "Sit in it and see how it feels. I'll go find the keys."

"Thanks."

Inside the office, I discovered my dad was a wizard of organization when it came to car keys. I found the Focus keys which were clearly labeled and returned in no time. I handed them to her. "I can't leave the lot right now, so you take it for a spin. Might not be much gas in it, so don't go too far." I knew that with used cars on a lot, no one ever left much gas in the tank.

I watched as she drove off, taking the turn onto the highway a bit tight and jumping the rear of the car up over the curb.

I began to wonder what had happened to my dad and Herman as I walked around the lot, waiting.

After a while, Kevin and Carew came back from lunch and made small talk with me about football, but I couldn't do much to keep up my side of the conversation. Then Faye was pulling back into the lot, bumping the front wheel up over the curb this time. Carew started to go out and greet her but I tapped my chest like an old pro at this and indicated this was my customer. Carew just smiled and allowed me to proceed.

"I'll take it," Faye said. "Can I get it today?"

"Um," I said. "Sure. That's great."

"What will you give me for my car?"

"Not sure. But we'll give it a look. My dad will be back shortly and we'll do up the paperwork."

I led her inside and made her a coffee. She seemed much less nervous now. "Thanks for this. I wasn't sure I could find anything I could afford."

"Glad I could help," I said, again pretending I knew what I was doing. And feeling rather pleased with myself.

When my dad arrived back in the Escalade, he and Herman laughed and shook hands, and my dad handed him a card. Then Herman drove off in his old Caddie. When Dad came in, I introduced him to Faye and explained that she wanted the Focus wagon and wanted to know what we could give her for her old car. Dad sent Kevin out to check out her car and sat Faye down with the paperwork.

I went back outside and, when my dad and Faye emerged a while later, she thanked me for being so helpful. "You're a lifesaver," she said. "I haven't had good experiences buying a car before and you made this so easy."

A short while later, she was actually driving her newly purchased car from the lot.

"You sold your first car, son," my dad said. "How's it feel?"

"Great," I said. "That was easy."

"Well, you did sell her the cheapest one on the lot," he added.

"It was the one she wanted. The customer is always right, yeah?"

He shook his head. "The customer is rarely right. But you did good. Did she even drive it?"

"Yep."

"Ouch," he said. "No license plates. Did you get a photocopy of her driver's license?"

"No. But she just wanted a test drive and I couldn't leave the place."

"You got a few things to learn," he said. "But I'll get you up to speed."

Another car had pulled in then and my dad walked away toward the new arrival. Despite his mild criticism, I felt good. Yep. I sold my first car and I felt like I had actually helped someone out. It felt okay.

chapter*twentytwo*

I sold one more car that first week. One. To an elderly man who was very hard of hearing. I didn't really sell it to him. He saw the Dodge truck on the lot and it was a deep shade of blue that he liked.

"That's the truck of my dreams," he said before I could utter one word of information about the three-year-old vehicle. "I'll take it."

The man said his name was Farley and that he wanted to pay cash. We went inside and my dad coached me through the paperwork. He got mad at me a couple of times because my writing was sloppy and I was bad at taking directions. Farley looked at me in a concerned way but didn't say anything.

Finally, the paperwork was done and my dad went out to greet another customer. I was to finish up with Farley.

"Sorry that took so long," I said to him.

He waved a hand. "I've got all the time in the world since my wife died. That man your father?"

"Yep. And my boss."

"That's a tough one."

I nodded. Things had started out well but I could feel tension mounting after Carew was fired. Kevin had been Carew's friend and he resented my intrusion. "I'm just learning the ropes," I told Farley. "I think I'll be fine." As I was talking to him, he studied my face like he was genuinely worried about me and I wondered why. That's when I realized he reminded me of my grandfather, who I had not seen in at least ten years.

"Well, I guess I need to pay you," he said, shifting the subject and standing up to reach into his pocket.

I handed him the sales sheet with the full amount and he put on his glasses and squinted at it. He pulled out a thick wad of bills and started peeling hundreds off of it. I'd never seen so much cash in one place and it made me think of my own fortune—what it would look like if it was sitting in a pile as real cash and not just a number in a bank account. There was a deep furrow in Farley's brow as he pulled off one bill at a time and began to pile them on the desk. "It's my wife's money, really. Life insurance. It was her idea, not mine. About me treating myself to a new truck, I mean."

"I'm sorry," I said again.

"Well, I miss her. She said that I should buy something I'd always wanted with the insurance money when she died. She said

I'd feel better." He stalled in his count for a second and then continued piling the bills. "But I don't. I like the truck and it's one I always wanted but could never afford. But it's not something I'm going to enjoy without her around."

I didn't know what to say. He finished stacking the bills and tidied the pile. "There," he said. "That should about do it. You should count it yourself."

But I didn't want to do that. "No. It's good."

I handed him the keys to the truck and he let out a deep sigh. "Well, at least I have the truck," he said and tried to smile.

I walked him out to his new vehicle and handed him my card. He looked at it like I'd given him a gift. "Still new at this job, eh?"

I nodded.

He held out his hand and I shook it. "You're a hell of a car salesman, bud," he said.

"Thanks."

Farley drove off and left me feeling oddly alone and abandoned.

When my dad came in, he saw the cash on the desk and smiled. "Good work, son," he said. But it was the last kind thing he said to me that day.

The rest of the afternoon was consumed with phone calls and what my dad called "complications." Sold cars that were giving customers trouble. A problem with the bank. Property taxes due. Car repair bills for clunkers being reconditioned for resale. On and on it went. I was on the sidelines but it wasn't fun to watch.

I didn't go to school at all that week. I hadn't told Carver that I had actually dropped out. But it was over, I knew that.

Kayla stopped by the car lot on Wednesday after school and let on that everything was okay with her, but she seemed nervous around my dad and apologized for coming to see me at work. "Come any time," I said as she was leaving, but that made my father frown. That damn frown of his was becoming awfully familiar.

The next day, Taylor picked me up after work and Kevin's jaw dropped nearly to the ground as he watched me get in her car. She gave me a present: a driver's handbook. "Brandon, you need to learn to drive. Study this. I'll coach you." There was that word again. "You pass this written test and you get a learner's permit. I'll pick the car you need and you'll be able to drive it as long as a licensed driver is along. That would be me. Or whomever you decide to date. Just make sure she has a license. But first we need to teach you how to kiss."

Taylor was always in charge and always full of surprises. By the time she dropped me off at home, I was rather blissed-out by the kissing lesson, but she insisted it was just that, a lesson and nothing more. "Learning to drive is just like learning to kiss," she said. This made absolutely no sense to me—but who was I to disagree? She gave me one final peck on the cheek and then slapped the book in my hand. "Read the damn book. Over and over. There will be a quiz the next time I see you. And I think you should call Chelsea. She's been asking about you."

My mom seemed rather happy when I arrived home but didn't pay much attention to me, just said there was food as usual in the fridge and that my dad would be home quite late that night. No surprise on either front. But she seemed more distant, and happier than usual.

I ate and retreated to my room—my fantasy world—to check text messages and e-mails. I had changed e-mail addresses and learned to filter out the unsolicited mail, but enjoyed those flirtatious messages from girls and women who considered themselves my friends, even though we'd never met. My liquor supply had been replenished and I'd sip a bit and then write an e-mail or have a live online chat with some of my favorite "friends." I knew I was wandering into a weird little fantasy world, but it was a world seemingly of my own creation and I was sure no harm would come of it.

By the time I was headed for bed, though, the bliss of the kissing lesson and the evening of online flirting began to wear off and I found myself thinking of Farley and the sadness in him over the loss of his wife. The even sadder part was thinking of him owning the truck of his dreams but no one to share it with. And that made me think of my grandfather, also a widower, who I didn't even know how to contact.

And then I had this weird vision of me—maybe it was the booze—but it was so real. I saw me as an old man, living alone in a big fancy house somewhere on an island with palm trees and warm breezes. But I was all alone and I was the saddest person in the world.

chapter*twentythree*

My dad insisted I work on Saturday and that sucked. Worse yet, I sold two fairly expensive cars, allowing him to say, "See, you put in that extra effort and it pays off." But nothing really paid off for me. There was no salary, it was explained, because I was a partner. No longer a silent, but an active partner. "So the better the company does, the more profit will be there for both of us."

But it was all wrong. Selling cars was not my life's work. By Saturday evening I was tired and sullen. I missed seeing other kids at school. I had to admit I missed some things about school. Not the work. Just the whole scene of being with people more or less my own age. And now that I was selling cars with my father, I had absolutely no sense of my own future. (Other than ending up as that sad old man in a posh house on an island.)

Sometimes when I went home, I would check my investments online—the ones set up for me by Les Cranmore, who I now dubbed "Less is More" because it turned out that mutual funds he had invested in had gone up in value by nearly two percent in the last couple of weeks. I discovered that this amounted to nearly $50,000. I was pretty sure this had to be wrong but I pulled out a calculator and went over the numbers. My money had made more money and I hadn't done a damn thing. I hadn't lifted a finger. So why the hell was I selling used cars?

That night I took Chelsea out on a date. Kind of a last-minute thing. I phoned her cell and she answered. I actually think she was already on a date somewhere with a guy but she didn't let on. Whoever he was got ditched in favor of me because Chelsea was at my door within a half hour. She was alone in her father's Audi and I could tell she'd been drinking.

When she kissed me, I tried to kiss her the way that Taylor had taught me and realized it wasn't quite the same feeling for me. When it came to kissing, Taylor was like an A-plus and Chelsea was a B-minus. But I didn't let on. Instead, I took a swig from the bottle of wine Chelsea had in her front seat. "Don't you know, you're not supposed to drink and drive," I told her, only half seriously. "It's in the driver's manual."

"Then I'll drive and you drink," she said as we pulled away. "Where to?"

"The Dome," I said. It was a nightclub near downtown.

"They won't let me in," she said. I was old enough and had my ID but Chelsea was a year younger and not old enough to legally drink or be allowed into bars.

"Yes, they will," I said. Taylor had coached me exactly how to approach the doorman and how much to offer. I took another slug of wine and smiled a big shit-eating smile.

We got in without a problem and I bought us some more drinks and we danced to the music, which was so loud we couldn't possibly have a conversation with each other. This was fine since neither one of us was great at conversations and we really didn't have that much in common. Chelsea took some pictures with her cell phone and before the evening was out, they were being circulated to her friends from school and appearing on Facebook and beyond. "It's all about social media," is the way Chelsea explained it. And I had kind of bought into Taylor's way of seeing the world. Buzz. Be cool. Look cool. Look uninterested. Be seen in the right place with the right people. That was the road toward adding the fame to the fortune.

Before the evening was out, we were both getting text messages from people on our phones about how cool it was that we were out on the town and how everyone wished they were us. It was late and I was starting to get tired, and I looked up from the screen on my phone at Chelsea. Yes, this girl was hot. No girl I knew was as sexy as she was—except, maybe, for Taylor. But here I was, sitting across the table from her. Yet it was like she was a million miles away. We'd both been sitting there for over a half-hour, communicating with people who weren't here and it was like we were not really with each other. How crazy is that?

That's when I sent a text to Kayla: HOW R U?

A few seconds passed and she was there: I'M OK. HOWZ UR DATE W/ CHELSEA? :(

Yeah, I guess everyone knew. But it was all a bit of a sham. There was no real chemistry between Chelsea and me. *ok*, I answered.

JUST OKAY?

YUP, NOTHING SPECIAL.

:), was her reply.

Taylor was trying to get through to talk to me on my cell but I didn't answer. It was too hard to hear and I didn't want to take any more advice from Taylor right now. Or maybe she was jealous. It was just all too weird.

When Chelsea let out an exasperated exhale at the next call coming in, I said, "Let's call it a night." I felt exhausted.

She nodded. I took her hand and led her to the door. A guy who had been gawking at her asked her if she would dance with him, but she said no. He gave me a dirty look and I gave him the un-affected, aloof, cool look Taylor had coached me on so well. It seemed to do the job. As we walked to the car, Chelsea leaned slightly onto me and she smiled. I liked the way I felt just then. A beautiful girl on my arm, out late at night downtown. The world was an amazing place.

We passed a couple of drunken guys taking a piss against the window of a Gap store. They said something rude to Chelsea but we kept on walking. I was not in knight-in-shining-armor mode nor was I meant to be that. I would just use the tools Taylor had taught me and they would serve me well. Cool. Aloof. Unaffected. Let the boys piss on the windows and be a little vulgar around my girl. Who cares?

I should have been concerned about Chelsea driving but I wasn't. She had a hard time getting the car out of the parking space but drove slowly and carefully, if a bit erratically, back to her house, all the while telling me how much she liked me and that I was "different" from the rest. I think she meant that I wasn't constantly pawing at her body, although the temptation was certainly there. I wasn't sure why we were in her driveway and not mine when she turned off the car.

"What's up?" I asked.

"My parents are gone for the weekend. You can stay."

A flood of images went through my head. Wild images. But then I discovered I was shaking my head no. "I gotta get up early in the morning. Something I promised."

"Please?" she cooed so softly and in such a sexy voice that I almost gave in.

"No," I said. "Sorry. It's important. I can walk home from here. Let me get you to your door."

What a gentleman I'd become. It shocked even me. But when I got Chelsea to her door and kissed her, she went playfully aggressive and tried to drag me into her house. I resisted as best I could, and eventually said goodbye and made her close the door.

It wasn't a long walk to my house but my mind was racing the whole while. I was both excited and confused. Sure, I'd just gone along for the ride tonight. I had the pretty girl, had the drinks, bribed our way into a club, sat back as the world watched us from afar as if we were celebrities, had the girl offer to have me stay the night. Who was writing this movie script? Whoever it was, I sure didn't want them to stop.

There were voices shouting inside my brain, telling me that I had arrived. It was all good. It was time to move forward. Take charge of my life. I was eighteen, not thirteen. Every part of that seemed exhilarating, but also somewhat frightening.

When I stopped at the big maple tree in front of my house and looked at the streetlight through the branches, I was feeling a confidence I had never felt before.

But by the time I quietly entered my old house and walked up the creaky stairs to my bedroom and heard my mother's voice, I lost every ounce of that confidence. She was standing in the doorway of her bedroom and had heard me come in. "Everything okay, Brandy?" She hadn't called me that since I was a kid.

"Yeah, Mom. It's all good."

"How was your date?"

"It was really nice," I said nonchalantly and then slipped into my room and fell into bed.

chapter*twentyfour*

On Sunday, I slept in and woke up to find a note on the kitchen table that my parents had *gone for a drive*. I think I knew what that meant.

I ate a sullen breakfast, went for a walk around the block to get the cobwebs out of my head, and then studied my driver's manual. None of this seemed very hard. Mostly traffic laws I was already familiar with, and common sense. It wasn't like that pointless crap they were trying to teach me in school. It got me thinking that pretty soon I'd be able to take the written test. Hell, I could do it this week if I was ready. Then I could drive with anyone who had a license. It was starting to click.

I called Taylor. "What are you doing?"

"It's called sleeping. Perhaps you've heard of it. What time is it?"

"Eleven."

"I'm surprised you're up."

"Yeah. I had fun last night. Get any reports about last night?"

"Reports? Are you kidding? There are photos and videos posted everywhere."

"Really?"

"Really. It's like you had a date with Paris Hilton. How'd it go?"

"Went okay, I guess."

"Looked more than okay. Looked awesome. I'm jealous."

"You were the one who set me up with Chelsea."

"Yeah, well, it was like you needed ... um ... training wheels."

I thought about that for a minute. "I don't get it."

"Training wheels. You know."

"Weird," was all I could say.

"Someone posted a video of you two leaving the club. You were kind of cool. But Chelsea looked a little wasted. The video shows you getting in her car and driving away."

That didn't sound good. "Who took it?"

"Dunno. Just some random person. That's the way it works if you're the center of attention. But you definitely seemed to have risen to the occasion. Did you sleep with her?"

"No."

"Why not?"

I paused. "I'm not sure." I didn't want to admit that I was a virgin. And I really wasn't sure why I didn't take Chelsea up on her offer.

"Anyway, that's probably a good thing," Taylor said matter-of-factly. She yawned. "So, what's on your mind that's so important you felt obliged to wake me up?"

"I need a car," I said. "You offered to help me pick out a car."

"Oh, so we're talking about shopping here." Now she seemed even more animated than usual.

"Well, I think I can ace this written exam and be on the road right away if I have someone to ride shotgun."

"That would be me. Give me an hour and I'll be over."

It took an hour and a half, but it gave me time to check out my presence on the Internet. I hadn't done a Google search on my name since the early days of winning the lottery. It was just too weird what people had to say. But I thought I'd see what was out there. In no time at all, I discovered Chelsea's phone photos, video clips taken by strangers in the club, and those clips of us outside on the street and driving away. All very public. And there were postings of people who had opinions on them and on me. *Hot guy*, was my favorite, posted by some girl. But there were others: *He looks gay*, was one. *What an asshole*, was another.

Funny how the negative ones stuck in my mind and the positive ones didn't. In the end, I began to think I might be better off not Googling myself. Let the world think what it wants to think. All those strangers out there didn't really know a damn thing about me.

I heard Taylor's car, then her car horn. Taylor wasn't the type to get out of the car and knock on the door. No way.

When I got in her car, she grabbed my head with both hands and gently but comically knocked it against hers. With her face close up to mine, she said, "You are coming along nicely," and then she laughed.

Once I'd recovered from that close encounter and buckled my seatbelt, I said, "I thought we'd go down to the car lot. It's Sunday and no one is there. You help me pick out the right car and then by tomorrow it will be mine."

Taylor frowned and then sighed. "I'm disappointed in you," she said, ever so seriously.

"Why?" I asked. I didn't get it.

"Your father sells used cars. You, Marlon Brando, need a *new* car. An expensive new car. Pick a letter."

"A," I said.

"A is no good."

"B."

"B is better," and she hit the gas as we drove off down the street.

The BMW dealer was open on Sunday, and the salesman, a very sophisticated man wearing a dark suit, seemed to recognize Taylor. At first, I was back to being invisible, until Taylor explained who I was and why we were there.

In no time at all, we were ushered into a dark blue car.

"Take it for a spin," the man said. "Keep it as long as you like."

And then we were back on the road. Taylor drove for a half-hour until we were out of town and then she stopped by a field with horses. "Now it's your turn."

"I don't know if I'm ready for this. And you know I don't have a license."

"Believe me, you're ready."

When I got out, I suddenly recognized where we were. I looked east and could see the tree. The tree I had climbed with Kayla. The one I'd fallen out of and nearly died. "Are you sure this is a good idea?"

"Yes," she said emphatically. "It's an automatic. No big deal."

And it wasn't a big deal. I drove.

There were no other cars around and, at first, I was very cautious, but then I speeded up a bit and, before long, it was like I'd been driving all my life. It seemed so natural. Why had I been holding back on getting my license for so long?

The guy in the suit walked out to greet us when we returned.

Before he could say a word, Taylor said, "We'll take it."

The man smiled and bowed like in an old movie. Inside his office, I wrote out a check for the entire amount and handed it to him. "I'll be back for the car later in the week," I said.

As we drove off, Taylor explained that her father bought all his cars there and that it would just be a matter of them cashing the check and then some paperwork. "Nothing to concern you," she said. "What day you gonna take the test?"

"Thursday," I answered. "I'll be ready by then." I heard the sound of my own voice and was shocked at the confidence.

chapter*twentyfive*

My parents were home by the time I returned. They were in the living room, sitting on the new furniture and looking at sections of the Sunday paper.

"Out having fun with your friends?" my mom asked, as if I was still a little kid out on his bicycle, riding around the block.

"Something like that." I sensed a tension in the room.

My dad smiled the car salesman smile. "Brandon," he began. "Your mother and I found the home of our dreams."

I guess I'd seen that coming. But, somehow, I had hoped this moment was going to be a long way off. And I knew my father. If he made his mind up that it was the dream home, he wouldn't back off. "You went to see it, right?"

"It's perfect."

I didn't like where this was headed at all. This totally sucked. "Two-car garage, right?"

My dad nodded.

"Pool?"

"In-ground. It's beautiful," my mom said.

"We put in an offer," Dad added right away.

Right around then, my day went immediately to crap. "What does that mean?"

"If the owners accept our offer, the place is ours. You won't believe the size of the bedrooms. There's even one with a fireplace. If you want that one, it's yours."

I was really pissed now. Something about the fireplace really nailed it. "I don't want a freaking fireplace in my bedroom," I said. And there was so much more to say but, instead, I just stared at my dad and then looked at my mom like she had betrayed me.

And I tromped off to my room, feeling like they'd both abandoned me. Right then, I wished I'd never won the money. I wanted my old life back.

There were family discussions that week and attempts to make everything okay. My mom did a lot of crying. My dad got more stubborn, saying that we were all definitely going to move and that I was too young to understand. I was accused of being selfish and immature. And maybe that was because I was selfish and immature. But it was my life, too.

I went to work on Monday and Tuesday and tried to avoid dealing with my father, but it wasn't working. Late Tuesday afternoon, he watched me put in a lackadaisical performance of trying to sell a red Mustang to a young accountant, and then he blew up at me.

"Brandon, you didn't even try. That guy wanted that car. All you had to do was tell him what he wanted to hear. It was a piece of cake. Snap out of this. Your mother and I want that house. The bank has already approved the mortgage. It's a done deal. I'm getting tired of putting up with your crap."

So it had finally come to this. "So what are you going to do? Fire me?"

He fumed but didn't say anything at first. "You were never like this before," he said, breathing heavily. "Drop the damn attitude. I'm not gonna take any more of it."

My dad was pulling one of his famous power trips on me. But it wasn't going to work this time. I'd had enough. "I quit," I said. "I'm not going to sell any more cars. And I hate the fact you're going to sell our house—the home where I grew up. And I hate the fact that you didn't take me into consideration about moving."

As I was about to leave the office, I stopped. I wanted to say something to hurt him. "Oh, and one more thing. I'm getting my driver's license after all. And I've already bought my first car. And it sure as hell wasn't from here."

And with that I left the office. When I was out by the highway, my father screamed something at me, but I couldn't make out the words and I just kept walking. It took me a while to figure out where I was going. I checked my watch: 4 PM. Yeah, she'd be home.

Kayla's mother answered the door and I asked if Kayla was home.

"She's in her room," her mom said, looking really happy to see me. "Why don't you go up and knock."

I did. Kayla, was happy to see me. The shades were down on her windows and it was rather dark in her room. "Hey," I said.

"Hey."

"You busy?"

"Not really," she said. "Just watching a documentary on the Internet."

"Is it any good?"

"Yeah. It's about quirky people who live and work in a scientific research station in Antarctica. But I can watch it later."

"Antarctica, huh?" Kayla would watch endless documentaries about just about anything to do with science or nature or space. She'd seen every documentary ever made about ants or snakes or fish.

"I'd like to live there," she said. And she was serious.

"Isn't it, like, really cold and really dark most of the time in the winter?"

"Yeah, but they have penguins there." As if that made all the dark and cold okay.

"Right, penguins."

"Brandon, what's wrong?"

I explained about the blowup I had with my father.

"You think they're really going to go through with it?"

"I think they already have," I said. "We're moving."

"But you don't want to move."

"Looks like I don't have much choice."

Kayla took off her glasses and polished them. I hadn't seen her without the glasses in quite a while. I'd known her for such a long time, and I can't say I'd noticed before how much she had changed. She had a kind of round, pretty face but she didn't look as heavy as I remembered.

"You lost some weight?" I asked.

"Yeah. A bit. I don't eat so much junk food and I stay in my room sometimes and exercise for an hour or so at a time."

"But you spend way too much time alone in your room here, don't you?"

"I like it here," she said, putting her glasses back on. That totally transformed her back into the geek that everyone thought she was.

"Kayla, what am I going to do?"

"I don't know. Would it really be that bad to move with your parents to this new house?"

"Yeah," I said. "It would really be bad. I've lived my whole life in the house that I know and love. I can't imagine another family living there."

"That sucks," she said.

"But I don't want to end up hating my parents, and I don't want my dad pissed off at me for the rest of my life. He wrote off his own father, I told you that. I never get to see my only living grandparent."

"You gonna go back to work tomorrow?"

"No. I knew that wasn't going to last. I just did it to try to keep my old man happy. But nothing I could do there is good enough."

"But what are you going to do?"

"Damned if I know. I can't just hang around the house all the time." And then I realized that, pretty soon, the house, my house, would no longer be part of my life.

"Thinking of going back to school?"

"No, I don't think so. School's not for me. Not now, anyway."

"Mr. Carver was asking me about you." Kayla rooted around in her schoolbag. "He wanted to give you this."

It was a piece of paper—school letterhead with Carver's office phone and home phone number written on it. "He said you should call him."

"He just wants to tell me how stupid I am for quitting school."

"Maybe not."

"It doesn't really matter. My life is starting to suck. Things looked good there for a bit but I guess that wasn't going to last."

"Are you kidding?" she said, now acting more like a cheerleader. "You've got amazing things ahead of you."

"It doesn't feel like that now."

"You need to take charge, Brandon. You're letting other people make decisions for you."

I must have scrunched up my forehead because it made Kayla laugh. The look must have reflected what I was thinking. The girl was dead on. Taylor telling me what clothes to wear, what girl to go out with, and what car to buy. My dad telling me what job to take and where to live.

"You're right," I said. "I don't really need to let other people make decisions for me all the time."

"No, you don't. You're eighteen; you have your own money.

You're smart ..."

I laughed. "Well, you got two out of three right."

"I could go on."

"That's okay. You made your point." I brushed her hair with my hand. I don't know why. I just wanted to show a sign of affection, wanted to indicate how much I appreciated the kind words. Her hair felt soft and alive.

Kayla blushed, but even as she did, she said this: "Why don't you make one important positive decision for yourself."

"Here? Right now?"

"Yes."

I thought about it for a minute. At first my brain was kind of fuzzy. I had never been good at making important decisions. Maybe because I was scared I would be wrong. But maybe the time had come.

And then suddenly the fog in my head cleared. The logic was there. The decision was obvious. "I'm going to buy my house," I said. "I won't have to move after all."

chapter*twentysix*

My father was home when I got there and my mother was a mess. He still looked angry but she looked heartbroken. I felt bad but I knew it was my time to create my own life. I'd have to make my stand.

"I know you guys really want to move," I said, "but it's not right for me. I've decided it's time for me to be on my own anyway."

"Brandon," my Mom said. "We didn't want this to happen."

I took a deep breath. "It's going to be okay." And then I looked at my father. "I don't want to argue with you anymore and I don't want to get mom more upset. But I don't want to sell cars. I'll go back to being a silent partner. You'll have to hire someone else. Someone who *likes* to sell cars. But there's more. I'm gonna move out for a while—rent an apartment. Something temporary.

I don't want to be around here while you two are packing up to move out."

"Brandon, please don't do this," my mom said, holding back the tears.

"Mom, you're going to love your new house. It's what you always wanted. I'll stay in touch. I'll visit. Like you said, you're only going to be twenty minutes away." I said that last part a little too sarcastically.

I turned back to my dad who seemed a bit stunned but much calmer. "And I want to buy this house," I said. "This is where I want to live." There. I came out and said what I had to say. And I really meant it. They could leave and go to hell for all I cared. I wanted to keep the home I had grown up in.

He looked even more stunned.

"Name the price," I said. "You guys take the new furniture and buy whatever else you'd like new for the new house. I'd like to keep most of the old stuff here, just as it is. I'd really like that."

It was like a bomb going off. Both of them had gone mute. "It will all work out for the best," I concluded, sounding like I knew what I was doing.

As I walked up to my room, I knew that I'd really miss my parents. It was like I was being forced to grow up overnight. Maybe it was about time. And besides, I was starting to think about my new life.

I e-mailed Taylor about helping me find a temporary apartment, and within ten minutes she had sent me a photo of a condo that was available by the month. Fully furnished, modern inside and out. And of course, it had a pool. "And indoor parking," Taylor noted. "For the Beemer." It turned out to be empty and I could move in any time I wanted. Immediately, if I liked.

While Taylor was in school the next day, I decided to scope the place out on my own. I'd been good at following her lead in grooming me for whatever she was grooming me for. But I was feeling a need to be a bit more assertive and do some stuff on my own. I contacted the owner, took a cab, and was shown the condo. The owner remembered me from the papers and seemed thrilled that I wanted to rent from him. He didn't seem to mind I was only eighteen. He knew I was good for the rent.

He showed me around. Two full floors. And somehow, I had failed to notice in the listing that it had a hot tub. I'd always thought hot tubs were kind of stupid. But now that I was about to live with one, I was thinking it was kind of cool. What girl could turn down an offer to come sit in my hot tub with me?

I signed some more paperwork and wrote another check. Having money seemed to be mostly about paperwork. Buying things. Agreeing to terms. Writing checks. Pushing a plastic card into a slot. Not really hard at all. And I was starting to like spending money almost as much as I liked winning it.

I took another cab to the school to try to find both Kayla and Taylor to tell them about my move. I'd never yet really told anyone at school I'd officially dropped out. Would it be against the rules for me to even be there? I didn't know. But it felt very weird walking into the building. I tried to remember where both girls would be at that time of day. But I didn't get very far before running into Mr. Carver. It was like the man was psychic or had x-ray vision. He walked up from behind and I nearly jumped out of my skin when he said my name a bit loudly.

"Brandon, welcome back."

I spun around. "Hey, Mr. Carver. Just visiting, really."

"We've missed you," he said. "*I've* missed you."

"I took a job."

"Oh?"

"Well, I *had* a job. I quit."

"Life on the outside not all it was cracked up to be?"

"I quit because I reminded myself that I didn't need to work." And then, for some foolish reason, I decided to tell him about how much I'd earned on my investments in such a short time.

"Got time for a short chat?"

I shrugged. "I guess." I still liked the guy, so I didn't want to be rude to him.

"My office is a bit stuffy. Let's go outside."

So we went out and sat on a low wall like a couple of school kids. "About investments," he began. "They go up and then sometimes they go down."

"I know that. My bank guy says he's going to be sure to preserve my capital."

"Those clever bank guys," he said, mocking me. "I hope you have a good one. But did I ever tell you about what I did before I started working here?"

"No." I saw a long-winded story coming on.

"Well, I was a hotshot stockbroker and an investment advisor. I advised other people on what to do with their hard-earned money."

"Like my bank guy?"

"Something like that. But I also had saved my money—my hard-earned money from a couple of previous jobs—and then, because I thought I knew what I was doing and because I was a hotshot stock wizard, I worked the market. Ever hear of day trading?"

"Not really. How do you trade days?"

He rolled his eyes. "I watched charts. These were the heady days of the NASDAQ. Dot com companies rising and falling. Lots of speculation. You familiar with that word?"

"Taking chances."

"Taking chances, for sure. With other people's money and with my own."

"And I bet you were good at it."

"The best. And also the most kick-ass, confident professional on the street. All I had to do was throw a dart at a wall listing new Internet companies and invest in that one. I would buy when it was very low, sell after a meteoric climb. Sell at a profit and watch my savings grow. Then pick another one and do it again."

"Sounds like fun."

"My clients loved me. My bank loved me. In a very short time, I had my own six figures."

"Really? No lie? I never thought of you as, well, wealthy."

"I'm not. That's the thing. My confidence was my downfall."

"Ouch. What happened?"

"You get cocky and you get greedy. When a smooth million is not enough, you think you can double it, triple it. But I invested heavily in a couple of 'sure things.' Never trust a sure thing, Brandon."

"And?"

"The bubble burst. The stock market bubble burst."

"How much did you lose?"

"Everything and then some. And I took a lot of my clients down with me. They lost houses—some lost marriages. I myself lost my job and I had to declare bankruptcy. One day I'm eating at the fanciest and most expensive restaurants around, and the next day I'm begging for change for a hamburger at Mickey D's. I've since become a vegetarian, but that's another story."

"So you decided to give up being a hotshot stock guy and day trader and sit behind a desk and deal with juvenile delinquents like me?"

"Yep. That's the short version. Although I wouldn't call you a JD exactly. But I share my cautionary tale just to remind you that your money may not always be there. Money—like women—like men—can be fickle. It is not reliable, no matter what smart-ass bankers say. It's comfortable, yes, but it is not your friend. So now, tell me, what are your plans for the future?"

"I bought a car. I'm getting a learner's permit. And I'm moving into a condo with a hot tub."

He lifted a brow. "You call that a plan?"

"Short-term plan."

"Very short. What else?"

"I haven't figured that out yet."

"But you're not coming back to school, are you?"

"No," I said. "School just didn't work out."

Mr. Carver stood up and let out an audible sigh. "Final word of advice for today. Working with people—helping people in any way you can—is much more rewarding than just working for money or spending money or living a life of leisure. Hot tubs aren't all that exciting after a while, believe me."

"I think I know that, Mr. Carver. Thanks for sharing your story."

"Thanks for listening. Seems like we get along better now that I'm not your vice principal. Maybe you'll stay in touch."

"Sure thing," I said, and I watched as he walked back into the school.

chapter*twentyseven*

I passed the written driver's test with flying colors. It made me feel that I wasn't as stupid as I thought I was. The trick was simple. I wanted to pass so I studied. I studied hard, despite all the other upheaval and distractions in my life. I wanted it that bad. Everything in my life had changed. I had changed. I would own my own house and I'd have my own car. So I worked at it. I studied. Maybe if I had applied those skills to school, I would have done better all along and never been left back.

When I came home and told my mom, she hugged me. "I guess you really are growing up now, aren't you?"

It seemed like a silly thing to say but I knew what she meant.

"Dad still mad about the car I bought?"

"A little. Are you still angry at us for wanting to move?"

"A little. But I think it's my time to be on my own. I'll stay in the apartment until you're all packed and gone and then move back here."

"Why don't you stay here with us until the move?"

I shook my head. "Nah. I think that part would make me sad and really drive me crazy."

"But you don't hate us?"

"No way. I just wasn't ready for all the changes that got started because of the lottery. Now I think it's all for the good."

"But what are you going to do ...?" The question trailed off.

"What am I going to do with my life? Is that what you're asking?"

"I guess that's what I meant."

"I'm going to live my life one day at a time," I said, sounding like I knew what I was talking about.

After dinner that night, my father and I discussed the technical details of me buying the house. The price. The process. What they would take and what would be left behind. What they wanted and what I wanted. It was all very civil and, for once, there was no bullshit. It wasn't like a father and a son, though. It was like two grown men, with mutual respect, hammering out the details of a rather complex business deal.

It was also the first day that I was officially renting my new apartment. I hadn't moved much of anything there but it was fully furnished, so what the heck. I told my parents I'd be around home off and on but that tonight would be my first night truly on my own. It felt totally awesome but maybe a little scary, too.

I thought about calling Taylor to give me a ride. Instead, I took a cab. On the way, we stopped at the liquor store and I bought some beer and a bottle of wine.

I arrived at my new apartment feeling a bit like a king. Everything seemed so new. I opened a beer, took a good long drink, and turned on the stereo. The heavy beat of the music blasted out sweetly from the speakers as I walked out on the balcony and looked at the manicured lawn beneath. The first night of the rest of my life. I had arrived.

And yes, I decided to try out the hot tub.

It was hot. And it was more like a small swimming pool than a tub. And I laughed a little when I turned on the jets and the water swirled and bubbled. But after soaking for about ten minutes, I was thinking about changing my plan of spending the night alone, just me getting to know my new apartment.

My first thought was to call Chelsea. She had been the first girl who had asked me to spend the night with her. Maybe she'd come stay the night with me. I sipped some more beer. Maybe this was finally my time.

But part of me was not ready for that. I liked Chelsea and she was so damned hot, but we were worlds apart. I expected if I called Taylor, she'd already be out doing something. Taylor wasn't one to be sitting home in the evening, watching television. If she was out, she might drop what she was doing and head on over.

But that didn't feel right either. There was really only one person I truly felt like hanging out with on a night like this.

So I phoned Kayla. "Whatcha doing?" I asked.

"Homework."

"Care to change your plans for the evening? Guess where I am?" I splashed some water around in the tub and flipped on the jets for just a second.

"You're in the condo?"

"Yep. Want to come hang out?"

There was a long pause and I wondered what that was all about. But then Kayla broke the silence and said, "Sure. I guess the homework can wait."

A half hour later, she was buzzing me from downstairs and I pushed the button to unlock the door and let her in the building. When she arrived at the door, I opened it and bowed like a character in an old play. "Greetings," I said.

I offered her a beer and she giggled like a little kid. I thought she was going to say no, but instead she accepted it. That beer was followed by a second and pretty soon we were reminiscing about stuff we'd done as kids. But before long, she turned rather serious and silent so I had to ask her what was on her mind.

"I've been skipping school a lot lately," she said.

"Why?"

"'Cause you're not there. I feel more lost than ever. I feel anxious all the time. It's like kids are looking at me. Judging me. Talking about me behind my back. So I'm faking being sick. My grades are slipping."

"Kayla, this is not like you."

"My doctor prescribed some anti-anxiety drug but I don't think it's working. I don't know if I'm gonna make it through the school year. Not without you there."

I looked at her and tried to figure out if this was some trick to get me to return to school or if she really meant it. "Kayla, it's your last year of high school. You can't just drop out."

"But I'm a mess. I have no friends. I'm scared all the time."

"You have me," I said and I reached over and gave her a hug.

"Thank you," she said.

And then I smiled. "I have an idea," I said.

"What?"

"We'll give you a new look. A makeover."

"Are you kidding? No way."

"Yes. Way. Tomorrow. But first, I want you to stay over to keep me company tonight."

"You want me to stay over?"

"Yes. And then we do the makeover tomorrow."

"Tomorrow is a school day," she reminded me.

"Then after school."

"But I'm just me. There's nothing you can do to improve me."

"You're great the way you are. But, with a little work and a lot of money, we can make you feel good about yourself and kids at school will look at you entirely differently." I guess I figured if Taylor could give me a makeover that transformed my personal image, then I could do the same for Kayla.

"This will never work," she said. "I'm not the type of person who can be made over. I am who I am."

"Yes, it will work. Trust me."

And that's when she gave up the resistance. "I trust you," she said.

The phone call to her mom went better than I expected. Her mother had always liked me. And trusted me. Kayla had put me on the line. "It's my first night in my apartment," I told her mom. "I've got two bedrooms. I'm feeling kind of all alone so I've asked Kayla to stay over."

Kayla's mom hesitated at first, but then I promised that we would be good and that I was feeling lonely and needed a friend. She paused, but then took a breath and reluctantly said okay. "Kayla's been spending way too much time alone," she said. "I guess it's okay. Just make sure she gets to school in the morning."

"I promise."

So Kayla spent my first night in my apartment with me. She did not sleep in the other bedroom, though. She started out there but pretty soon came to be with me. We both slept with our clothes on. But before we went to sleep, I phoned the limo service for her ride to school in the morning.

"You've got to be kidding," she said.

"This is just to get you in the right mood for the makeover."

"Thank you, Brandon," she said. But she did not try to kiss me.

In the morning, the limo driver rang from downstairs and Kayla was off to school as promised.

In the afternoon, the limo picked her up again and then came for me. We went to the mall, to the stores that Taylor had mentioned to me—the places where she shopped. We both needed coaching from the sales people, but they were all so anxious to swipe my credit card that it wasn't too long before we had the wardrobe, then ordered some new glasses (with the discussed possibility of contact lenses), and finally made a trip to the hair salon where she received the royal treatment.

When we arrived back at Kayla's house and her mother took one look at her daughter, she let out a howl of delight and hugged her. And who said money can't buy happiness?

chapter**twentyeight**

On Saturday, a taxi took me to pick up Taylor. The driver, a heavy-set man with a big gold chain around his neck recognized me from the papers. "You're that lucky-ass kid, right?"

"That's me," I said, getting in. I had become used to the recognition by now and wondered when it would start to fade.

"You know what I'd do if I had all that money?" he said.

I'd heard that line plenty of times before. "What?"

He waved his hand in the air. "Nah. I shouldn't say. It wouldn't be polite."

I didn't say anything so he picked up the slack anyway. "Well, the one thing I can say out loud is that I wouldn't be sitting on my ass fifty hours a week driving this sorry-ass car and taking crap from strangers."

"I can understand that."

I directed him to Taylor's house, and when she walked out the door and started walking toward us, the driver said, "Holy Mother of God, would you look at that?" I smiled. "She your girlfriend?" he added.

"Nope. My driving instructor."

"I ain't never seen no driving instructor who looked like that," he said.

"We're headed to pick up my new car," I told him. The dealer had promised to have it detailed, prepped, waxed, and ready to roll. As Taylor got in, she kissed me once on the cheek lightly as the driver took in the show in his rearview mirror. I told him the location of the dealer and we drove off.

The BMW was sparkling and smelled new, as only a new car like this could smell. "It's intoxicating," Taylor said as we got in. I started it up and checked the side mirrors and adjusted the electric seat. "Everything's electric," I said, a little surprised.

"It's a luxury car. You're not supposed to have to work at anything."

"But I still have to steer it, right, and use the gas pedal?"

"Yes."

I was glad the car was an automatic. I wasn't ready for the five-speed standard that had first been offered. I took my time pulling out into traffic and just driving down the road. Taylor was looking into the little mirror behind the sun visor, checking her makeup. I said, "I can't believe I'm driving my own car."

"Believe it, Brandon. Where should we go?"

"I don't know. Can't we just drive?"

"We should have a destination. Let's go back to the beach."

"The beach it is," I said, discovering the button on the dash that controlled the sunroof. It was a cool but clear day, and I liked the feel of the sunlight on my shoulders. Taylor looked up at the sky and laughed and then turned on the heater to low. "Brandon, you're starting to adjust to your new life. I see confidence where there was once none."

I just nodded like I already knew that. I took my time as I drove, thought through each lane change, carefully put on my turn signals, and made perfect turns. I admit, it was like the car almost did drive itself, but I felt good about the fact I was a being a competent driver. I knew I was new at it and really needed to keep my wits. I couldn't believe I'd put off driving so long. As long as I was careful, I figured I'd be okay. Nothing fancy. Just basic driving.

Taylor put some music on and we cruised along with some serious volume, not talking at all, but then, as we got closer to the ocean, she turned it off. "Chelsea's feeling ignored," she said. "You haven't called her for a while."

"Didn't you tell me that cool was all about not caring, or at least pretending not to care?"

"Then, you do care about her? Just playing a little hard to get?"

I hadn't really thought about it that way. "Not really," I answered. "I'm just not sure about the chemistry between us."

"Brandon, she's just about the hottest girl in the entire school." Taylor didn't need to add the part about herself being the hottest.

"Don't get me wrong," I said, with the sound of ultimate cool in my voice, "I like her."

"That's good. I was getting worried there for a minute that you might be gay."

"I'm not gay."

"But you are a very funny person."

"Why funny?"

"Unpredictable. You ignore Chelsea but you take your old girlfriend, Kayla, out on the town to buy her a new look."

I kept my eyes straight ahead on the road. "She's never been my girlfriend. Just a friend. And a good friend at that."

Taylor scrunched up her pretty face. "Well, she sure looked different. You guys didn't exactly get the whole package right, though. In fact, some of my friends thought it was hilarious—Kayla trying to look like that. But it was an improvement."

What Taylor had said struck me as condescending and cruel. Why did it shock me that she would say such a thing? What would Kayla feel like if she knew that some of Taylor's friends were laughing at her? Suddenly the old Brandon was the one sitting there in the driver's seat, wondering how he ever got there—how he got the car, and this beautiful girl beside him.

Taylor noticed that I was quiet. "Did I say something wrong? Hurt your feelings?"

I wasn't going to let on. I smiled. "'Course not. I was just concentrating on the road." But when we got off the highway and hit the first red light, I put my arm around Taylor, pulled her to me, and gave her a serious kiss on the mouth.

She poked me in the ribs when the light changed. "Where'd that come from?" she asked, not sounding the least bit offended.

"Just making sure you didn't think I was gay."

"Proves nothing," she said joking. "I hear gay guys can really kiss."

We never really made it to the beach. As we neared the ocean, Taylor looked at the digital clock on the dash. "It's time for lunch. We need to celebrate. You have your credit card this time?"

I gave her a hard look.

"Great. I know the place."

"The place" was Three Fathom Restaurant and it had a dining room overlooking the ocean. It also had a guy in the front in a uniform who parked your car. I handed him the keys. "Don't scratch it," I said. "It's brand new." The guy looked thrilled to be able to park it.

Inside, Taylor asked for a table near the window. The place was nearly empty and we were directed to our seats. As we were sitting down, Taylor asked, "Could we see the wine list?"

The waiter nodded and returned with one for each of us.

"Do you think this is a good idea?" I asked.

"Of course," she said. "You're still learning the ropes. I need to teach you about how to order the right wine with your meal."

I was thinking about the driving afterwards but I didn't want to sound like a party pooper. "How do you know what the right wine is?" I looked at the complex and rather confusing wine list, which was as big as a menu and covered four pages. I'd never once in my entire life worried myself as to what the right wine for a meal would be.

"You look at the price, silly."

So I looked at the prices. The cheapest bottle was $30.

"Red or white?" she asked.

"Doesn't matter to me."

"Red then."

"French, Italian, Australian, South African, or Chilean?"

"French," I said, trying not to sound like too much of a lug nut.

"I can live with that. How about this one?" She held out her wine list and I saw her pointing to something with an unpronounceable name. And a price tag of $120.

I'm sure my eyes widened, but then the new me kicked in. The cool me. What the hell. "That looks good to me," I said.

Taylor put a single finger in the air and the waiter breezed quickly and silently to our table. The deed was done. A bottle ordered, and elegant wine glasses appeared at the table. A small amount was poured in her glass, not mine. She tasted and approved. When the waiter poured some in my glass, I took a sip and found the taste rather unpleasant, if not downright obnoxious.

I guess the look on my face was a bit obvious. "It's a bit dry, isn't it?" Taylor asked. "Do you want me to send it back?"

"No," I said. "It's fine."

So fine that I ended up drinking half of the bottle. Well, maybe more than half. Taylor had ordered us what seemed to me to be the most expensive food on the menu. There were escargot. (I thought she was joking but they really were snails.) And there was some dish made from goose livers. (Although it had a French name and I didn't realize it was goose livers until I had already eaten most of them.) And there was something else involving mushrooms. "Chanterelles," Taylor had said. "I totally adore chanterelles." (Me, I've never been a fan of mushrooms of any sort.) So maybe this all explains why I drank so much of the wine.

But we had a fine view of the ocean and Taylor seemed to be loving every minute of it and, due to the glow from the wine, I suppose I was feeling like the king of the world. I remember that I became rather talkative and began telling her funny stories about when I was a little kid and thought I could fly. I would continually jump out of trees—from not too high up—and test my flight abilities, only to fail over and over. I had always believed that if I thought about it hard and long enough, it would happen.

But it never did.

"And then one day, I find myself sitting in a fancy-ass restaurant with the most beautiful girl in North America, eating snails and drinking red French wine." There was no clear connection to the story but that's how I ended it.

Taylor laughed so hard she almost choked and the waiter came running. But she was okay. And I settled back into being the less extroverted version of me.

The bill was over $300 but I didn't blink. It was play money, after all. And the wine had gone to my head so it was worth it.

The car was brought to us and I noticed the air had become much cooler. There would be no open sunroof for the ride home. "Are you okay to drive?" Taylor asked.

"Absolutely," I said.

I was aware of the laws about drinking and driving but was pretty sure that didn't apply to a couple of people having a little wine with a meal. Otherwise, why would they be able to sell wine to you with a meal? It had to be okay. And, in fact, as I got behind the wheel and headed us home, I felt even more confident in my driving than before. If anything, the wine had turned me into a better driver. I was more relaxed and more focused.

Taylor put on some quiet music and started telling me some things about her childhood. Her trips with her mom sounded exotic at first, but then it became clear she had spent a lot of her time alone while growing up with two very busy parents. "And then the boyfriends kicked in," she added.

"How many have there been?"

"I've lost count," she said. "But I'm not trying to brag. It's just that not long after I get involved with the guy I'm interested in, well, I seem to lose interest."

"That's too bad. So what do you do?"

"Move on to the next one."

"And there's always a next one?"

"Always."

As far as I knew, though, there was no obvious boyfriend in Taylor's current life. She had explained fully to me, however, that she saw herself as a kind of "mentor" to me. She had no real "interest." I thought about asking her if her views about me had changed. It seemed clear that she liked me and she liked being with me. But I decided not to push my luck. I looked straight ahead at the road.

When things got a little too quiet in the car, I looked over and saw that she was leaning against the door of my BMW and had fallen asleep.

chapter***twentynine***

I talked to my parents on the phone at least once each day. I may have moved out and I was still mad at them, but I wasn't going to forget the fact that they were my parents and they had raised me. My mom was all flustered with details about moving. I talked mostly to her, since my dad was often working late and seemed not to have much time to talk to me if I called him at work. According to my mom, there were a lot of complications with the business that were troubling him. She wasn't sure he was really making any money at all, but then my father had explained to me that it could take a while before the business actually turned a profit. My dad, however, when he had a spare minute or two to talk to me, told me everything was fine.

"I finally found what I was looking for. His name is Sidney.

He loves selling cars and the customers love him. Sidney could sell anything to anybody. He and I have been moving a lot of inventory."

"That's great, Dad," I said. But I think it was maybe an exaggeration, and I also took it as a kind of jab at me for not being a super-salesman. Oh, well.

Life on my own was sometimes good and sometimes not so good. After a couple of weeks on my own, though, I was starting to adjust. Kayla helped me buy groceries and I bought her some more clothes and makeup. She thanked me for the new look and told me that guys were actually starting to pay attention to her at school. I felt a little funny when she said that. Could it be that I was jealous? No way.

Kayla had been inspired by the new image to lose some weight as well and she was looking much different from the girl I used to climb trees with. She said she still experienced anxiety attacks and, if she was home, she'd call me and ask if she was interrupting anything. Usually she wasn't. A couple of times she called at night, when the anxiety set in, and she asked if she could come over. I always said yes. She'd stay the night. She said she'd had a long talk with her parents about sleeping over and they had said it was okay. They understood and, strangely, they said they fully "trusted" me. They probably didn't know that we'd have a couple of glasses of wine or some beer. But Kayla would always be ready for school the next day and we really didn't get into any trouble. Taylor dropped in from time to time—but never when Kayla was there—and we'd go for drives in my car or occasionally to one of the clubs.

And Chelsea. Well, Chelsea called me often. And she'd drop by without calling first. And she was still one of the sexiest girls from school. I was flattered that she wanted to be with me. And I had grown to believe that it was more than the money. But I could have been wrong. Chelsea liked to party. Chelsea liked to drink vodka coolers and she liked to smoke a bit of weed. She liked to turn the music up loud and she liked to sit in the hot tub with me. And sometimes it went a little further than that. We had some of the most amazing times together. She was never shy about anything. Let me just say that it got pretty wild sometimes. And I loved it. And if she stayed over, she didn't always make it to school the next day.

Since Chelsea now had her full driver's license, we two would go for drives. Chelsea in the morning, however, was different from Chelsea at night. The girl was moody and, in order to cheer her up, I'd take her to the mall and buy her some new clothes. I was amazed at how much time I spent in clothing stores since I'd moved into my new life. But I didn't mind. And it did cheer Chelsea up. And, after all, it was only money.

I tried discussing Chelsea and Taylor with Kayla. I wanted to be super honest and open about everything. But that didn't work.

Kayla was shaking her head. "Look, I just don't want to hear about it. It's just too weird. I need you, though, Brando. So if I call you and Taylor is here 'coaching you' or whatever the hell it is she does, or if Chelsea is here getting high, just let me know and I won't bother you." She was trying not to sound angry but she was angry.

"I know it's all kind of weird, I guess. Not quite normal. But this is just the way things have happened. It wasn't like I planned it. I'm sorry. But I'll be here if you need me. I promise. How are things going at school?" I asked, trying to change the subject.

She took a deep breath. "Better," she said. "I can't believe people treat me differently because I look different."

"Sometimes it works that way."

"And I got asked out," she said sheepishly with a half-smile.

I had mixed feelings ... which surprised me, but I said, "Excellent. Who asked you?"

"John Gardner."

"The guy from the school newspaper who ran an editorial against my promoting gambling and greed?"

"He's very political. I wouldn't take it too personally."

"He said I was encouraging people to become gambling addicts and ruin their lives," I said a bit too loudly.

"He does get carried away. But he has very high ideals."

"He's an asshole," I said. I remember how I'd felt after the article.

"He's been nice to me. We'll see how the date goes."

"Do you mind my asking where he's taking you?"

"To see a documentary about child soldiers in Africa."

"How romantic," I said with a bit too much edge in my voice. I really didn't like the idea of her hanging out with John Gardner.

Kayla wrinkled her brow and took off her stylish glasses. She really had changed in some subtle way that made her so very different from the girl I used to climb trees with. "You're not jealous, are you?"

"No way," I said. And for some reason I repeated it. "No way."

In two weeks my parents would move into their new house—their new lives, as my mom was now prone to say. I had offered my parents a more than generous price for our old home. In two weeks, odd as it seemed, I could move out of my fancy-ass apartment and back into my home, a home which would be truly mine to do with whatever I wanted. Only now, that was starting to feel a little too weird. And even sad. Living there all alone.

Taylor kept saying that before I moved out of the condo, I needed to have a party. This was seconded by Chelsea.

Kayla was the first person I invited. Well, she was the only person I personally invited.

"I'm not coming," she said.

"You can bring John," I countered.

"I only went out on one date with him. And it wasn't like a date. It was more like a lesson in morality. But he was nice."

"Bring him. I don't care if he insulted me back then."

"No. The party thing is a bad idea."

"It will be cool."

"It will be trouble."

And that was the end of that conversation.

But things were already in motion at that point, Chelsea and Taylor drawing up the guest list, making the appropriate invites on Facebook, etc. Taylor ordered some food and booze. I paid for it all, of course. Hell, I'd never thrown a party before.

"Get on good terms with the neighbors above you, below you, and on each side ahead of time. You want them to like you. Tell them things will be controlled and not too loud."

I did this, offering a bottle of white wine to each of my neighbors, as planned. They all looked a little strangely at me, but I quickly learned that as soon as I told them who I was, they seemed to soften. "One night only," I promised them. "This won't be a regular thing." At least one couple, Steven and Wanda Richards, who owned an interior design business, invited me to stop over some time for dinner. Everything was cool. Taylor knew exactly how to handle these things.

"It's all about diplomacy," she said, the afternoon before the big event.

Taylor and I split a bottle of wine around five o'clock the night of the party and ate some pizza as we made the final preparations. Music, food, booze. I was thinking that maybe this was another step on the path to my adjusting to being wealthy. Sure, I was only eighteen, but I sure didn't feel like a teenager anymore. This was the life.

The party was supposed to start at seven but no one showed up until 8:30, which gave Taylor and me a chance to share some more wine. Chelsea was the first to arrive with Brittany and Emma. Chelsea wrapped her arms around me and buried her face in my neck. I saw the look on Taylor's face—the smirk. I knew what Chelsea was doing, staking out her territory. I liked the hug though and I could smell that she'd been smoking weed. So what else was new?

Within a half-hour, it was clear that a real party was in full progress. Some of Chelsea's pot-smoking friends arrived and she lost interest in me as she followed them out onto the balcony for a few puffs. I thought maybe I should be worried about other residents calling the cops, but the wine had gone to my head and I wasn't much worried about anything. Everyone else had gotten into the action fairly quickly. But then, that was what a party was all about, right?

At first, everyone was shaking my hand, patting me on the back, and thanking me for inviting them. (Although I didn't invite them.) Even Grant Freeman, apparently, had been on the invite list.

"That whole ruckus back then was my fault entirely," Grant said. "I wanted so badly to be you. Forgiveness?"

"Forgiveness," I said. What the hell.

That's when Grant dropped his pants and tore off his shirt and jumped into my living-room hot tub. He flicked it on and a minute later Brittany had taken off her blouse and skirt and joined him.

I was a little shocked, but then I'd never partied with these people before. I wasn't about to join them. But it was the first true sign, my fuzzy brain concluded, that this was not *my* party at all.

chapter thirty

Chelsea came back in when she saw a couple of others jump into the hot tub. "Shall we?" she said.

"Not me," I said. I'd been drinking but I wasn't that drunk. I wasn't about to go parading in my underwear in front of all my old classmates.

She looked a little disappointed but did not go in the tub on her own. Instead, she held onto my arm and whispered loudly into my ear. "This is the best party I've ever been to. I am so glad that you're my boyfriend." She pressed up so tightly against me and that felt really good.

But was I really her boyfriend? The way she said it sounded not quite right. Like it was rehearsed. It didn't seem real. Taylor had set Chelsea up with me. It was great but was Taylor maybe running a bit too much of my life? Looking around at my apartment, with kids drinking and some dancing and some standing on my furniture, (why were they standing on my furniture?), it all suddenly didn't seem exactly right for me and my life.

Grant had gotten out of the hot tub and was dripping all over the floor as he walked first to grab a beer from the fridge and then to my bathroom where he put on my bathrobe. As he waltzed back into the living room, still dripping under the robe, he looked like he owned the place. I'd let it go. If I said one word to Grant, he'd flip. Then disaster would follow. Be cool, I told myself. Be cool and try to enjoy yourself. I was suddenly glad Kayla was not here to see this.

I switched from wine to beer so that I wouldn't get too drunk. It could be a long night. The first beer went down pretty smooth and it was followed by a second one. Someone had turned the music up way too loud and I turned it down a tad, hoping that no one would notice. Chelsea and Emma seemed to be having a very serious conversation—most likely it wasn't about child soldiers but nail polish—and I didn't want to intrude.

When I found Taylor, she was talking to my personal hero, Grant Freeman.

"Love the indoor pool, Brandon," Grant said. He meant the hot tub. "Always wanted one. My stingy parents were always too damn cheap." Grant's parents, I think, owned a bank or something like a bank. "Now, this is the life."

Taylor was laughing as he spoke. She was clearly enjoying herself and sipping some more wine. There were expensive snacks set out on the counters and my former classmates were feasting, although there were a number of people here whose names I didn't know and who I didn't recognize. The room was stuffed with bodies. Taylor now seemed more interested in Grant than me, and Chelsea was still deep in discussion about whatever, so I figured it was my time to tour the room and introduce myself to some of the fine-looking young women I did not know.

I was awkward with the first one but, as soon as she understood who I was, everything changed. That made me more confident with the second and third. And then a girl named Stephanie, who I had never met before, said she'd been dying to meet me. She said she'd crashed the party after hearing about it through the grapevine. And she told me she wasn't a student really. She'd graduated high school and was now a model for a "very important agency."

I then recognized her as one of my "fans" who had appeared via e-mail after I'd won the lottery. "I'm glad you came," I said. I really was glad. At least at that moment.

She opened her purse. "Here's one of the pictures from my portfolio."

I took the picture of her in a bathing suit, a very skimpy bathing suit. "My phone number is on the back."

"Gee, thanks," I said. No kidding. I used the word "Gee." Just like a little kid.

"You have a great place."

"It's nice but temporary. I'm moving into a house I bought in a couple of weeks. This is sort of a goodbye party to the condo." I didn't tell her it was the house I grew up in.

"You don't mind that I crashed?"

"Not at all. It's great to meet you."

"You're sweet," she said. "I don't really know anybody else here. Would you hang out with me?"

"I'm not sure I really know most of these people either." A quick look at Taylor and Chelsea again convinced me that neither had much interest in whether I was having a good time. And the truth was, aside from meeting the gorgeous young woman who was now talking to me, I wasn't really having that great of a time at my own party. I looked at Stephanie and she looked back at me like she'd just met the most important person in her life. That's when I blurted it out. "Do you want to take a break and go for a ride in my car?"

"Sure," she said immediately.

Without an ounce of fanfare—or interest from the other party-goers who were really going at the party—we slipped out the door. Soon we were seated in the BMW and on the road.

"Where would you like to go?" I asked.

"Anywhere, as long as it's with you," she said, slipping her hand into mine.

I found myself driving past my father's used car lot. Although it was closed, the sign was brightly lit and I saw my last name in those huge letters. Then I drove by my old house and on past where Kayla lived. I could see that there was a light on in her room.

Stephanie asked me some things about myself. She seemed intelligent and sensitive and a little deeper than Chelsea and less pushy than Taylor. I was thinking that there were possibilities here.

Maybe it was time for me to choose my own girlfriend. "How old are you, Stephanie?" I asked.

"Twenty-three," she said. "You're eighteen, right?"

"Yep."

"Does it bother you? The age thing?"

"Nope."

"I like younger guys," she said, making me wonder how many there had been. But I felt like she really liked me. I felt different with her than I felt with Chelsea.

"I like being with you," was all I could follow that with. I turned to look at her and I guess I must not have been careful enough with my driving because I let the car slip ever so slightly across the road and a driver coming the other way lay heavily on his horn.

"Oops," I said. "I better stay focused. It's a new car. I'm still getting used to it."

Unfortunately, not much more than three minutes later, I saw the lights of a police cruiser flashing behind me and heard the siren. I pulled over immediately and started to panic.

I looked at Stephanie and saw fear in her face.

"Shit," I said out loud.

A flashlight was in my face and a knuckle was knocking on my window. I rolled it down.

"License and registration?"

I dutifully handed them over. I was staying very cool. I was sure this would all be over very quickly and it would all be okay.

"This is a learner's permit," the cop said. I still hadn't had a look at his face. "She a licensed driver?"

I had not said a word about being a new driver to Stephanie. I looked at her. "Sorry. Could you show him your license?"

Stephanie gave me a baffled look. "I don't have a driver's license," she said.

I froze. I don't know if she was lying or if she really didn't have a license.

The cop said to me, "Can you step out of the car?"

I took a deep breath and got out.

I could see now that he was a clean-cut, muscular man of about thirty. "Have you had anything to drink tonight?"

"No," I lied.

"You're just learning to drive, right?"

"Yes. I have the learner's permit."

"But you passed the written test?"

"Yes."

"Do you remember the part about drinking and driving?"

"Of course."

"Do you always slur your words or only when you're drinking?" he asked with an ominous tone in his voice. I truly didn't think I was slurring my words. But it was sinking in that he could obviously tell that I'd been drinking.

I'd never ever been in trouble with the law. And I had this feeling that if I ever got in the slightest trouble, I'd be polite and apologize and the policeman would be kind. He'd give me a little lecture and I'd promise never to do whatever again. And that would be the end of that. "I had one beer," I said, thinking this would make everything okay.

"Turn around, please."

I turned around and suddenly felt hard metal clamping down tightly on my wrists. "You'll have to come with me."

With that, he pushed me toward his police car and sat me down in the caged back seat. There was police chatter on the radio. And static. I remember lots of static. He closed the doors and then I saw him talking to Stephanie who had stepped out of my car. She had a cell phone up to her ear. I was hoping she would look at me or come over or offer some kind of explanation or assistance that would get me out of this predicament. But she didn't. She looked completely in the other direction and talked on her cell phone and then to the police officer, who was asking her questions.

And then I watched as he took my keys from the car, walked back toward me, and sat back down in the front. "Isn't this all a bit unnecessary?" I asked.

"It's the way we do things these days. I pulled you over because there was a complaint from another driver. They phoned in the description of the car. You were the only BMW on the road going this way. Car's in your name, too. Thought it would belong to Daddy."

"I bought it myself."

"Nice," he said.

That's when a cab stopped and I watched Stephanie get in. She never looked back at me once. The arresting officer must have felt obliged to explain why she was let go or maybe he wanted to rub salt into my wounds. "She said she'd just met you. I asked if she wanted to accompany you to the station until this was settled. She said no. She was free to go. You comfortable back there?"

I felt like crying but held it together. I said nothing.

Pretty soon a tow truck arrived and the cop handed him the keys to my car. After that, he drove me to the police station. It was going to be one hell of a long and difficult night.

chapter*thirtyone*

The handcuffs were tight and they dug into my wrists. All I kept thinking was: *This can't be happening to me!* But it *was* happening to me. It's possible that it wasn't until that moment, handcuffed, sitting in the caged back seat of a police car, that I realized just how much the alcohol had affected me. I'd been drinking wine and beer ever since Taylor had first arrived. Going for a drive was a supremely bad idea.

But right then, at that minute, there was absolutely nothing I could do about it. I had gotten myself into this mess. And Stephanie had simply bailed on me. Who could blame her?

At the police station, I was led into a very brightly lit room. "We'd like to give you a blood alcohol test using a breath analysis machine. You care to call a lawyer?" he asked.

"Yeah," I said, "I think so."

"Go ahead," said, handing me a desk phone.

"I don't know who to call," I said.

"Want me to dial Legal Aid for you?"

"Yes," I said.

He dialed a number from memory and held out the phone.

When a woman answered on the other end and introduced herself, I told her my name and explained my predicament. Then I asked the question, "Can I refuse to take the test?"

"You can," she said matter-of-factly, "but the punishment will be the equivalent of your being found guilty of driving while under the influence."

I was not ready at that point to even ask what the punishment would be. "So the best option is just to take the test and hope for the best?"

"Probably," she said.

"Thanks," I said. And hung up the phone. "I have to pee real bad," I told the cop who arrested me.

"Sure," he said. "Follow me."

I followed him to a small bathroom and went to close the door behind me but he put out his foot to stop me. "Sorry. But I can't let you be in there alone. I need to stand here with the door open."

I think it was then that I truly believed I had wandered out of reality and into some really cheesy bad cop reality show. But I had to pee, so there I was standing in front of a toilet with a cop watching me pee. How weird was that?

Afterwards, I was led into another brightly lit room and

introduced to another police officer and his Breathalyzer machine.

"I'm Stephen Coombs," he said rather casually, "and I'm going to test your blood-alcohol content. Ever done this before?"

"No," I said, the full weight of the moment starting to catch up with me.

He held out a tube. "Well, you blow a good lungful of air into this tube and then I'll get a reading on this machine."

I hesitated to take the tube.

"It's easy," he said sarcastically. "But if you burp, we have to wait fifteen minutes before we test you. Otherwise it throws off the reading."

As if on cue, I had to burp.

"Okay. We have to wait. Want to tell me anything about yourself?"

"Not really," I said.

"How much did you have to drink?"

"One, maybe two beers."

"That's what they all say."

I looked down at the floor. After a little while, I burped a second time. Coombs checked his watch. The policeman who arrested me hovered nearby. It looked like he was writing out a report. After some time passed, I burped a third time. "Sorry," I said. "I didn't do it on purpose."

Coombs looked at the other cop and they both rolled their eyes.

So I made a point of not burping anymore.

Finally, Coombs handed me the mouthpiece again. I blew into

it. He wrote down a reading.

Not long after, he took a second reading.

Looking at a printed read-out he said, "You're well over the limit. Blood alcohol content of 0.05."

After that, the first cop took over again. He handed me some paperwork. "As of now, you no longer have a beginner's driver's license. And it's gonna be a long time before you can even apply for one again. You'll find out all about that later." He handed me a legal-size yellow form. "This paper here states you were driving under the influence of alcohol. You've been charged. And you are to appear in court on the date stated there. Do you understand?" He asked that last question like I was a little kid. A bad little kid.

I nodded yes.

Another phone was handed to me. "Call someone to pick you up."

I must have looked at the phone like I'd never seen one before. My mind was a muddle. I was scared. I was confused. And the beer and wine had me feeling both buzzed and very, very tired. I tried to think rationally.

I should have called my parents.

But I didn't.

And I couldn't call Taylor or Chelsea on their cell phones. If either one of them or anyone else from the party showed up, that would just make things worse. The cops would end up busting my party. The one that was probably still going on at my place without me there.

I thought about calling Kayla.

And I should have. Even if it meant her coming here with her parents. I should have done that.

But I didn't.

"Let me call a cab, okay?" I asked.

"Sorry," the arresting cop said. "I can't let you do that." Then he looked frustrated and ran a hand through his short cropped hair. "Look, we've wasted enough time on you already." And, with that, he shocked the hell out of me by putting the cuffs back on me. "Come on," he said.

"Where are we going?" I asked.

"You'll find out."

We went down two flights of stairs, me stumbling once and almost falling, except he was hanging onto my elbow.

A uniformed woman in another brightly lit room asked me for everything from my pockets.

"Belt?" she said. "We need your belt."

I took it off and handed it to her.

"Watch?"

I gave it to her.

"Wallet?"

I handed it over.

"Shoe laces?"

"You've got to be kidding." I said

"Not kidding."

I took the laces out of my running shoes and handed them to her. She asked me to sign a document. I signed it without reading it. Panic was settling into my head but everything around me was fuzzy.

Next, I was led through the jail. My first image was of a young man, maybe twenty-five years old, standing at the front of a cell, completely naked, holding onto the bars. Some men were in group cells and looked up at me as I walked by. Some were obviously drunk and shouted at the cop who led me.

It was the real thing. A jail. I walked past the shouting men, some kicking at the bars. It was like some terrible nightmare. I kept wanting to say, "There must be some mistake." But there was no mistake. This was reality. This was my life. I had got myself into this. I had screwed up really bad. All I wanted was to be out of there.

As I stumbled forward, I began to wish I could turn the clock backwards. I wished I was still a kid, living at home, still going to school. Yeah, waking up in the morning from a bad dream and getting myself ready to go to school.

Fortunately for me, I was led to my own private cell. Four feet by eight feet. I walked inside. The door closed with a heavy metallic clang. And I was locked in. No one had said anything but I knew I was there for the night. Possibly more. I was in jail. Holy Christ.

Then the cop was gone. I had two concrete walls on either side of me. If I sat sideways on my bed, I could brace my feet against the far wall, it was that narrow. The floor was concrete and one caged light bulb hung from the ceiling. There was no one in the cell across from me. I felt isolated and alone.

I sat down on the hard stainless steel shelf that was to be my bed. Beside it was a seatless stainless steel toilet attached to a sink. But when I tried to turn the water on at the faucet, nothing came out. I was very thirsty. But it looked like the only water to drink here was from the toilet. And that wasn't going to happen.

I lay down on the steel bunk and tried to calm myself as the panic began to set in. I felt nauseous and almost threw up a couple of times. But I didn't. My watch had been taken. I had no idea what time it was. And no idea how long I would be held here.

There were no police officers walking by to ask for water or to ask about the time.

I felt very, very alone.

And then another prisoner who I couldn't see in the next cell beside me began screaming something unintelligible. It was a horrible, unearthly scream. He began kicking hard and relentlessly on the cell door. Maybe he was crazy violent, maybe he was on drugs. I'd never heard anything like that before. I lay on my back now, closed my eyes, and tried to make everything go away.

It didn't.

Another prisoner from nearby screamed at the first screamer to shut up. An argument followed. A really angry, stupid, pointless name-calling argument between two men, with me invisibly sandwiched in my cell between them. I remained silent and squeezed my shut eyes tighter. I tried again to make it all go away.

chapter*thirtytwo*

I'd never before been in serious trouble in my whole life. The worst thing I ever did was accidentally break a neighbor's window while playing backyard baseball as a kid. I'd never imagined myself arrested and thrown in jail.

But here I was.

I was dead tired but my mind was racing. Was my apartment trashed by now? Was the party still going? Did anyone notice or care that I wasn't there? Would Taylor take charge and make sure everything went okay? But that was the least of my worries.

And Kayla. Kayla had told me not to have the party. Kayla was wise. Why didn't I listen to her?

What would my parents say when they found out? And they would find out.

I found myself thinking of Stephanie. I had really liked her. Did she do what she had to do by calling a cab? Could she have helped in the situation, helped me? Did she really have a driver's license and lie so as not to be drawn into my problems? Maybe she saw me for what I was. A screwup. Trouble. I took out her picture. It was in my shirt pocket and I had failed to leave it with all my other stuff. I stared at it. A very beautiful young woman who had been interested in me. I turned it over and looked at her phone number. I almost laughed.

But the fear and panic was setting back in. I wondered if this was what Kayla felt like when she had her panic attacks. I reminded myself that I was the one creating the panic in me. In my mind. All I needed to do was control it.

Further away, there was another loud, angry man having what sounded like an argument with himself. Then the image of the naked young man, his face contorted and pressed up against the bars, came back to haunt me. I began to see that I had one small bit of good luck with me tonight. The cops had decided to lock me in my own private cell. Oh, my god. What would it have been like to be locked up with the naked guy or the shouting, insanely angry men?

I sat up again to stop the racing thoughts; I put my back up against the cold concrete and my feet up against the opposite wall. My entire world was whittled down to this. All I had to do was get through the night. If I was lucky, they'd let me out in the morning. I just needed to keep myself sane through the night.

I failed to fall asleep at first, but eventually faded off a little; the light was very bright and, just when it seemed to get quiet in the jail, someone began to scream again. And again.

When I heard the first screaming voice of a woman, I realized there were women housed in cells at the far end of this basement we were in. A woman screaming a name. "Darren! Darren!" she wailed at the top of her lungs.

And then Darren answered. A raw, raspy shout from the guy next door who had been screaming and kicking his door. "Carla, is that you?"

At first, I almost thought it romantic. Two drunk crazies, both arrested and shouting at each other from opposite ends of the jail. But it wasn't like that.

"Darren, you stupid piece of shit!" she screamed for everyone to hear. "Look what you got us into!"

Darren wasn't about to take the insult quietly. "Shut up, Carla. I'm gonna break your face when we get out of here!"

Nope. No romance at all. It went on like that for fifteen minutes, along with other jailbirds shouting out for them to shut up. If I wasn't feeling so desperate, I might have actually laughed out loud.

When things settled down, I faded again but did not really sleep. Someone else started shouting out, "What time is it? Does anybody know the time?" But none of us had watches. And there were no police walking up and down through the cell block. None that I saw. Like the others, I wanted to know what time it was. There were no clocks, no windows. And no water to drink. And it was getting harder to control my mind, my panic.

I took several deep breaths. I remembered something I once

learned from a magazine about self-hypnosis. I concentrated on relaxing every part of my body. Then my mind. Then counting backwards ten to one. But just about when I'd get there and just about when I relaxed enough that I thought I'd fall asleep, Darren or Carla or someone else would let out an unearthly shriek or curse, and I'd be wide awake and fully aware of where I was.

Keeping myself sane was my most important task.

I remembered back to days from my childhood. The good days with my parents. Car trips to the parks, the beach, the mountains. The trees. I started to picture the green of the leaves of trees. And then I was climbing them. It was a long time ago. Kayla and I were maybe twelve. She was above me in a crabapple tree we'd discovered in an empty lot.

I closed my eyes and climbed tree after tree. I could not see her in my visions but I knew I was not alone. A shadowy but reassuring someone was always there in the tree above me or below me. And there was sunlight, bright sunlight sifting through the branches.

I guess I did finally fall asleep but I don't know for how long. The human wails and howling had stopped. I was out of it. But then, suddenly, I must have sensed myself falling. Falling like in those childhood dreams when you're falling out of the night sky and you wake instantly as you feel you're hitting hard onto the surface of the earth.

I woke up at that instant and sat bolt upright. I didn't know where I was.

My mouth was dry and my head was fuzzy.

And I was in jail. It was all real.

I think things got harder after that. I was still tired and my back ached from sleeping on the hard metal. I tried to calm myself again but I couldn't. I felt cold and scared and I started to shake, then sat there with my knees scrunched up, hugging my legs. This was bad, a voice in my head kept saying. Very bad.

But there was another voice. I can't say I recognized the voice but I like to think it was the voice of my father. In recent years, he had been so caught up in his ambitions and his work and then the new business that there had not been a lot of warm father/son moments. But he had been different, once upon a time. Back before his falling-out with my grandfather. Back when I was young. I think it was the voice of him back then that I was hearing. "You will get through this, Brandon. Everything will be okay."

I heard this voice more than once. And when it receded, I waited for it to return.

And I did get through it.

One by one, the other prisoners were escorted from their cells when what must have been morning arrived. I seemed invisible to the attending policemen, so I finally piped up in a croaky voice to one walking by, "What about me?"

He looked puzzled, as if they had truly forgotten I was there. "I'll check," he said.

When I was finally allowed out and given my watch, it read 1:30. It was the afternoon. I was given back my other things and freed to just leave. Once some more paperwork was signed, it was as if the attending cops suddenly lost all interest in me. I had to ask where the door was to leave the building.

"Down the hall and up the stairs," one said and laughed a little.

I stumbled out into the cool bright afternoon and stood there by the side of the road for a minute. I looked at the police station that I'd seen maybe a hundred times before in my life, never knowing what went on inside. The panic was gone. I'd survived my night in jail.

A small bubble of euphoria at being free came over me. But it was quickly pushed down by the fact that this was not over. There would be a fine, a court appearance. And God knows how this might affect the rest of my life. Maybe I'd never be allowed to drive my new car or any car.

I started walking, realizing that I had never been prepared for the chain of events set in motion by winning the lottery. Maybe Mr. Carver was right. But maybe it wasn't the lottery at all. Maybe I just wasn't ready to be living in the adult world. My legs ached as I moved forward. The air was chilly and I only had a thin jacket. A thin, very expensive jacket. I saw a taxi and considered flagging it down, but decided I should just keep walking. Even though I didn't know where I was going.

My befuddled mind came to the conclusion it was Saturday. And I realized there was only one person I should go see right now. I wasn't going to go back to my condo just then to see what the partygoers had left of the place. No, I decided I'd go to the one person who might be able to help straighten me out a little.

chapter*thirtythree*

Kayla answered the door and immediately knew something was wrong. "Brandon, you look like crap. What happened?"

"I spent the night in jail," I said.

Her eyes were wide but she didn't speak.

"Can we go for a walk?" I asked. "I'll tell you all about it."

"Sure," she said. "Let's go."

As we walked, I told her the whole sorry tale. She didn't tell me "I told you so." She just looked very concerned and then suddenly stopped and gave me a hug. "You'll get through this," she said.

"I don't know how I could be so stupid."

"You're human. Things moved too fast. Now you need to regroup."

We were in front of the public library. There was a low wall by the sidewalk and I sat down on it. Kayla sat beside me. I took a deep breath. "I really screwed up. I'm gonna have to go to court.

Everyone will know. I'll have to pay a fine. I may never get my license now. And I'm going to have to tell the truth to my parents. They'll kill me. But, you know, as bad as all that is, there's something else that's bothering me more."

Kayla sat silently and studied me. I could see how deeply she was worried about me. "What's the something else?"

"I just don't know who I am anymore. I don't know what I want, and I don't know who my real friends are, and I don't know where I'm going." And then I started to cry. Yeah, I cried. Kayla held me again as a couple of elderly women walked by and stared at us.

"Maybe you should go live with your parents for a while. Give yourself some time to chill out."

I shook my head. "Not in their new home. I'd hate that. I've hated everything about them wanting to move. That would only make things worse."

"Well, then maybe when you move back into your old house, things will settle down and you'll feel grounded."

She was trying to be helpful, but maybe nothing really could help me right then. I'd crashed and burned. In jail, I'd felt like I'd nearly lost my mind. "I'm worried about that, too. It won't be the same. It will be like a shadow of my old life. My parents gone. A lot of the old familiar things gone. What will I do? Sit in my room and make new friends on the Internet? It's going to suck, I know." I blew my nose and felt embarrassed at what a mess I was. "Kayla, would you come stay with me? Live with me for a while?"

Kayla put her arm around me. "You're tired, Brandon. You've

lived through hell. You need sleep." She paused and drew back a little. "I'll come visit you. I don't think I can live with you."

Despite the fact that Kayla was here for me and being the best friend anyone could be, I was beginning to realize that something about her had changed. Something about *us* had changed. I was afraid to say that out loud. I decided to change the subject. "How are things in *your* life?"

I could tell she wasn't sure how to answer. When your own life has gone completely down the toilet, the last thing you want to hear from someone else is how well their life is going. Yeah, maybe I wanted her to tell me what a lost soul she'd been without having me around school and hanging out with her more often. Instead, she answered with one word. "Better," she said sheepishly.

"I'm glad," was all I could muster. I looked at her face for a few seconds. I studied her. The glasses, the hair, the clothes. My advice and gifts had made a difference in her. But it wasn't just that. She was a different person. The schizzy look in the eyes was gone. The slouch was missing. Beyond her concern for me was an air of confidence. Someone who was not afraid of the world. I now didn't want to hear any more about how things were "better." I was afraid it would open up a wider chasm between us. And, right now, I needed her badly.

"So what do you do now?" she asked. "Today?"

I decided it was time to stop wallowing. I'd have to face up to all the crap ahead eventually. But for now, I had to get on with my own life, see if I could pull myself together, and begin to repair whatever damage I had done.

"Come back to the apartment with me?"

"I don't know," she said. "Do we have to go there? What if there are people from the party still crashed out there? What if the party is still going?"

I knew I couldn't face going back there on my own and I was starting to feel panic rise up in me. I just wasn't ready to face any sort of new problem today on my own. I needed Kayla. I guess my face said all that. My lips didn't need to move.

"Okay," she said. "I guess I can. But I'll have to go in the library first and make a phone call. I didn't bring my cell. I need to tell someone I can't make it for what we had planned."

"John Gardner?"

"Yeah. He'll understand. I won't tell him why. Stay here. I'll be right back."

Kayla walked into the library and again I was alone with my thoughts, tangled and convoluted as they were. *Just get through today,* I told myself. *Don't think about the future. Not even tomorrow. Find one small thread to hold onto for now. Hang onto that until you've had a rest and can think straight.*

And that one small thread was Kayla.

The condo had been royally trashed. There was water from the hot tub all over the place. Bottles and cans scattered around the floor. Leather furniture stained and ripped. The refrigerator door was open. In the bedrooms, it looked like a war had taken place. But the partiers were all long gone. There was a foul smell to the place, and I discovered the toilet had been plugged up and that, too, had flowed out onto the floor. I wanted to cry again. But didn't.

I went to the sink and poured myself a large glass of water. I realized I was dehydrated and feeling nauseous. As I stood there, leaning against the kitchen cabinet, Kayla went into the smelly bathroom and grabbed some towels. She threw them onto the water on the floor, pulled the drain plug on the tub. Then she started picking up bottles from the floor and putting them into a box. "Nice friends you have," she said, letting some real hostility slip through in her voice. Mad at them, yes. But also mad at me for being such a stupid shit to let my life come to this.

The look on her face was fierce determination and anger. She picked up garbage, mopped the floor. I started stuffing leftover food and garbage into a garbage bag. I found a couple of used condoms just lying there on the floor. My new life, I was thinking. My new, stinking life. Kayla watched with disgust as I picked them up with a paper towel and threw them into the garbage bag.

I really wanted to just crawl into bed and fall asleep. I wanted Kayla to lie there and hold me until I woke up and could begin to piece myself back together. But the bedroom was a disaster. Everything was a disaster. When Taylor and Chelsea and all the rest had left, they obviously had no thoughts in their head about me and what I'd come home to. They would not have known I was in jail. Maybe they thought I'd sneaked off with that young woman, Stephanie, and deserted my own party. Maybe Chelsea or Taylor was really pissed at me and this was done on purpose.

Or maybe no one had noticed I was even gone and they partied until the place was trashed. I tried to stop thinking about it as I yanked the sheets off my bed and found another used condom.

At that point, Kayla and I were working away at the chaos in different rooms. I needed to stop and talk to her before the silence between us made me crazy. When I left my bedroom, I found her in the bathroom with rubber gloves on, hauling full rolls of toilet paper from the shit-dirty water of the toilet bowl and putting them into garbage bags. The look on her face said it all.

I swallowed hard and said, "I'm sorry. I should have cleaned this all up myself."

Kayla flushed the toilet then and it worked. She grabbed some more towels and threw them onto the dirty, wet tiled floor and then ripped off the rubber gloves. "Brandon," she said with a new fierce edge to her voice, "if you don't make some hard decisions in the days ahead, that's going to be you, flushing your life down the toilet. When you started hanging out with Taylor and then Chelsea, I felt really hurt. Those two had always treated us like we were dirt. And then things changed for you. I got over it but I felt abandoned. I watched you let them draw you in, attach themselves to you, change you, mold you, use you.

"And you accepted it all without question." Kayla's eyes were wild now. "You claimed to still be my friend and maybe you were. But, for me, it was like I'd lost the one good thing in my life. And recently, even though you and I still talked to each other, still hung out, everything kept shifting. And I tried to go along with it. I really did. Taylor's remake of you. Then you, having learned from the expert, trying to remake me. Into what? Something more acceptable to them? Maybe I liked being me. Sure, the whole world scared me. I was trying to hide out from it. But maybe a smart part of me didn't really want to be part of that shallow, mindless world."

"Kayla, I'm sorry. I didn't know that's how you felt."

She took a deep breath. "Brandon, I'm not going to say anything more. I've said too much already. When I came here today, I promised myself I would not get mad at you, but I couldn't help myself. I know you're feeling weak right now, but you needed to hear it. And I'm not sure anything can be the same between us again."

I couldn't bring myself to say anything. I felt a hollowness well up within me.

Kayla was washing her hands now. "You need to sleep," she said. "You're exhausted." Then she went into my bedroom, kicked at the pile of dirty sheets on the floor, found some clean ones and made the bed. She nodded to the bed. "I'm going to just sit out on your balcony for a bit and get some fresh air until you get to sleep. Then I'm going to head home. I'm having a hard time just being here. I'll let myself out after you're asleep. When you wake up, find something to eat. Then call your parents. I think you need to tell them what happened. The sooner the better."

As I climbed into bed, I felt a great wave of sadness and defeat wash over me. I wondered how my good luck could lead to so much loss and hurt. I beat myself up for screwing things up so badly. I cursed myself over and over.

And then I eventually just stopped caring and gave myself over to the blissful unconsciousness of sleep.

chapter*thirtyfour*

My parents were still at our old house on Sunday, and when I arrived there, they were packing dishes in the kitchen into boxes.

I told them a short version of my story as I stared at the floor.

My dad went through the roof. To him, driving an automobile was like breathing or eating. "You're old enough to drive and now you've already maybe screwed that up for your entire life," he said.

My mom was a little kinder. "At least you didn't hurt anyone," she said. "But why didn't you call us to come pick you up?"

"You need to move with us to the new house," my father insisted, once he began to cool down. "You obviously need someone to rein you in, keep you from messing up your life even further."

"I can't do that," I said. "I'm moving back here. This is where I want to be."

My mom looked really worried. She looked to my father. "Maybe we should put off moving into the new place until things settle down with Brandon."

But my father shook his head. He looked at me as he spoke to my mom. "No. Brandon wanted to have his freedom—he needs to learn about responsibility. And he needs to do it the hard way, I guess."

My father was right, but he hurt me deeply by saying what he said just then.

I felt like leaving but I didn't. My mom unpacked a couple of pots and plates and made a Sunday dinner for me and my dad. It would be the last meal we'd have together in the house. The silence was broken after a bit by my mother reminiscing about good times we'd had in this home. My father dropped the anger and joined in with his own memories. And so did I. And then I said this: "At least the old place will always stay in the family and you guys can come over once in a while and I'll cook for you." It was a way of telling them I would forgive them for moving on to a new home. I may not have known it then, but I guess I was beginning to realize that if I wanted people to forgive me for screwing up I was going to have to learn to forgive them, too.

I knew I had to get a lawyer to help me do whatever I needed to do about my legal problem. I wanted to keep my dad out of that though, so I called Mr. Carver at home and asked him to give me some advice. He said he was sorry I'd got myself into so much trouble but that he wasn't surprised. "It's not just you, Brandon.

It's human nature. You moved into a new way of living too fast. You need a plan. A good plan. But first you need a good lawyer. You going to try to fight this?"

"No," I said. "I was guilty."

"Good. I like that. First thing anybody needs to do is own up to the truth. Pay your dues and move on."

"I just don't know what to move on to."

"That's not going to be easy to figure out. But use this thing. Use this problem as a way of starting to move on."

"I don't understand."

"You will, I think. You're not the first person on earth to screw up badly. The trick is the recovery. It ain't easy but it builds what we used to call character."

So Mr. Carver referred me to a lawyer, an expensive lawyer. "You might as well put some of that silly money to good use," was his way of saying it.

I'm not even sure I needed a lawyer because I was pleading guilty, but Josh Kellogg was probably just what I needed. He explained everything I needed to know. He answered every question and when the time came to go to court with me, he stood beside me as the prosecutor described the arrest and the judge asked for my plea. "Guilty," I said. And guilty I was. Mr. Carver was in attendance that day and so were my parents.

The fine was hefty. The lawyer's fees were insane. And I wouldn't have a chance to even have a learner's permit for a long time. But I could get on with my life. If I had a life.

Chelsea had seen me leave the party with Stephanie and that really pissed her off. She told Taylor and then Taylor was equally pissed off at me. She had lost control of her pet project. I was a wild card, a free man who had just walked away on them for an older girl. Who the hell did I think I was?

Which helped to explain the state of my apartment. And aside from a couple of really nasty cell phone conversations from both girls, that was the end of that. Suffice it to say that whatever positive reputation I may have had at school was trashed as successfully as was the condo. I had the wrong notion that one or the other of them might cool off and want to hang out with me again, but that wasn't going to happen.

Taylor's final e-mail to me was this: *You got what you deserved.*

Chelsea just never communicated with me again.

I guess if a guy sits around in a fancy apartment long enough by himself, he'll call almost anyone to ease his loneliness. That's what I discovered late one evening when I called Stephanie. She was more than a little shocked to hear from me. "Want me to come over?" she asked, after hearing my sorry tale and realizing how desperate I was.

"Yeah," I said.

She did come over and she apologized for abandoning me that night and said she really had a driver's license, but didn't own up to it because it would have meant she'd be charged as well.

And she pretended to really like me for a while until she discovered I was about to leave the apartment and move back into my old house. "That's kind of creepy," she said. And then things went quickly off the rails. She started saying that I was too cheap with my money. That I should be having more fun with it. What she meant was that I should be spending more of it on her.

And I started doing that for a while.

And she seemed happier with me.

And then I did a little test. I stopped being quite so generous with meals and presents and guess what?

She lost interest.

And Kayla. What about Kayla?

Kayla began spending more time with John Gardner. She would still take my phone calls when I sounded desperate. And she stayed over at my apartment a couple of nights to keep me company. She even apologized for not having as much time for me as before. I missed her badly.

But it was clear she didn't miss me. "If I could have the old you back, I'd love it. But that's not going to happen."

"I know," I said sadly.

Kayla and I had both changed.

So it was not a particularly exciting day when I moved back into the home that I had grown up in. My parents came over and I cooked them a roasted chicken dinner. Yes, living alone had taught me to cook. But it was a little awkward. And sad. And, maybe Stephanie was right, a little creepy. When my folks left to drive home to their new house twenty minutes away, it seemed like they were leaving for another planet. I felt more alone than ever before.

Which is why I phoned a cab to drive me in the other direction out of town. The cab driver was a little surprised when I asked him to drop me off in the middle of an empty field. "It's okay," I said. "Just going for a hike." I gave him a big tip and he was more than pleased.

I walked off into that field, my jacket tight around me. Any warmth left in the air was now gone and, almost without my noticing, the tail end of summer had slipped into fall, and fall was headed toward winter. I could see my breath in the air. The sky was sullen with low gray clouds. The sun broke through now and then as I walked, but it was quickly swallowed up by the clouds again. At least there was no wind.

When I came to the tree, I almost didn't recognize it. The leaves were all gone; the branches looked gnarled and unfriendly. At first it seemed impossible that I could even get up to the lowest branch. But I did.

I had to jump three times. The third time I got a grip on the rough bark. And I struggled to pull myself up. I was breathing heavily at that point but I went higher. And higher. When I located and sat down on the very branch where I had once found myself sitting before, I closed my eyes and found myself hugging the trunk of the old tree. I felt panic and true fear as I stared far down at the ground.

Once my breathing calmed and I got my brain under control, I took my cell phone out of my pocket and dialed Kayla's number. I wanted to tell her where I was, although I'd never be able to explain why I was there.

But, of course, there was no signal. I held the phone out and above my head. Still nothing. So I put the phone on camera mode and held it at arm's length and took a picture of myself.

A boy. A rather wealthy young man, really. But still a boy. Sitting high up in a tree.

Alone.

Many things were not clear to the boy in the photograph. All he knew was that he wanted to sit there for a long while, not thinking about the past. Not thinking about the future. And wait for just the right inspired moment to climb back down and find his way back home.

Interview with **Lesley Choyce**

Your young adult novels usually feature characters who are loners, as Brandon is, but they're also usually gifted, intelligent individuals who are ahead of the game. In this case, your principal character doesn't have these qualities. What interested you in Brandon?

I was thinking about those rather average teenage guys who are just cruising through their lives—emotionally a bit immature, not great at school or sports, not terribly social, not greatly inspired or passionate about much. They don't hate their lives; they just don't have high expectations of good stuff happening to them. So Brandon was that young dude. And I wanted to see what he did if something big happened and it changed his life dramatically all at once.

So, as usual, I put myself in his shoes and did the necessary authorial thing. As I was writing, I became Brandon. The upside is that I got to win three million dollars. Yahoo. But I knew it wasn't going to be an easy ride for us. Brandon just wasn't prepared for what it would mean. How could he be?

And therein was the seed for what I thought would be a challenging but intriguing story.

Winners are not always winners — in fact, winners can be losers. Is this what Brandon has to learn?

Sometimes when you win, you lose. I know I've heard that line before somewhere but it is true. I did my research into lottery winner horror stories and it was quite enlightening. Winning large amounts of money or any form of coming into lots of money unearned tends to create real disasters for many people. So I was thinking about how difficult it would be for a eighteen-year-old kid who is still in high school. Once I dropped Brandon into his new role as a wealthy teenaged boy, I watched him make all the likely mistakes and followed him into his struggle to ... well, survive in the new world he was trying to create for himself. It's a monumental struggle.

One of Brandon's disadvantages is that he seems to have no enthusiasms, no areas where he feels he can excel in life. Do you think there are a lot of teenagers who suffer from this lack of focus?

I think a lot of us are "lost" at various points in our lives—young or old. I feel sad for anyone who hasn't found some strong set of passions to live by. At the beginning of the story, Brandon is floating through life. I've heard people speak about winning the lottery as solving all their problems and that it would be a dream come true. But most of us will never win big in a lottery so it's just a silly notion not worthy of pursuit.

Poor Brandon now has a number of things to cope with that he is not prepared for:

1. He has "friends"—including girls—who mostly only want to be with him for his money and his notoriety.

2. He can drop out of school and forget about even tentative plans for more education and job training. Why bother?

3. He can now almost fully be an adult—buy a car, rent his own apartment, buy whatever he wants—without having been prepared for these responsibilities.

4. And much more.

The young man is in real trouble.

Brandon wants to be part of a group, likes the idea of having acceptable friends, going with "hot girls." Is this a major cause of his downfall?

We all want to be accepted. We all want friends and we want to be attractive to others. The best we can hope for is that people are attracted to us for who we really are. Brandon has found himself in a very false, shallow, and delusional world. He's on a downward spiral although, like many, he's having some fun along the way. The big question posed in the book is, how can he find his way out of the downward spiral? It isn't going to be easy. What skills can he learn along the way to save himself? The book hints at answers but doesn't give any easy solutions.

I'm interested in how you select names for characters in your novels. Can you tell me how you came to the names of the major characters in this story?

I've written so many novels and have used so many character names that this is not easy. This will sound like cheating but here's what I do to ensure my names are contemporary.

I figure out the year the book will likely be published and subtract the age of the character to determine the year that most teen characters were born. Then I Google the popular baby names for that year. I rarely choose the most popular ones but look at those in the 10 to 20 range and select the ones that resonate the most for the characters I am creating.

What is the significance of the fact that the two characters who really sympathize with Brandon—Kayla and the vice-principal—are both outsiders, in a sense?

I really like Kayla—she is sincere, smart, and a good real friend to Brandon. Even as older teens, they still like to climb trees. She helps ground Brandon but is losing out to the temptations of his new life. And she is definitely not part of the in crowd at school or anywhere else. But they are good together and Brandon can't truly see how important she is. So now she is even more of an outsider but she has strengths that Brandon does not have.

I have a strong affinity to outsiders and have been one myself for much of my life. We sometimes create the very reasons that make us outsiders. Truth is we don't necessarily *want* to fit in. We want to be fiercely independent. And we pay a price for it.

The vice principal, Mr. Carver, is a unique example of a smart, compassionate man in a position of authority who knows how to use his job in the school to help guide young people. He knows what it feels like to be an outsider as he is black and he is gay. He is a good ally for Brandon but Brandon is too caught up in his new whirlwind to be able to recognize him as a good friend and mentor.

Could there have been an alternative story where the windfall of cash is truly a blessing for a eighteen-year-old and sets off a chain of very positive life experiences?

Perhaps there is an alternate tale to be told about how instant wealth was a truly good thing for a teenager. Maybe the winner would recognize the power of money to do good deeds and create a means of channeling it towards just that. But it would take an extraordinary person of great strength and wisdom beyond his years. Most of us don't really figure out how insignificant money is in our lives and in the big scheme of things until we are much older. The sad truth is that too much success, too much fame, or too much money at too young of an age is a very dangerous thing. Nonetheless, I do believe there are some out there who had great fortune early on and handled it wisely. And for them it would have been the result of far more than just good luck.

Praise for *Lesley Choyce*

Random

"The story has plenty of dramatic activity. . . What many teens may enjoy even more than the plot specifics, though, is Joseph's unpretentious search for meaning that emerges from his "random thoughts," which range from Malthus to Buddhism to Aristotle to his namesake, Joseph Campbell, who, in describing the mythic hero's perilous journey, articulates what may feel like coming-of-age concerns for many teens."

—*Booklist*

"With Joseph Campbell, Lesley Choyce offers readers a young male character who is complex, intelligent, and (dare I say it,) sensitive. *Random* is a "must-buy" book for high school libraries, and an absolute "must-read"... make it a deliberate acquisition!"

—*CM Magazine*

Living Outside the Lines

"Choyce has written a beautiful story that will draw readers in to its possibilities."

—*School Library Journal*

"Lesley Choyce offers teen readers a tantalizing vision of the future that raises many challenging and thought-provoking questions in this book that is both highly engaging and easily accessible. . ."

—*Atlantic Books Today*

The End of the World As We Know It

"Carson's story of subtle growth and quiet transformation will resonate with a wide range off readers. It is a beautifully honest book tinged with sadness, but ultimately filled with optimism and hope."

—*Atlantic Books Today*

"Each character in Lesley Choyce's novel is clearly profiled and dons a prevalent issue facing today's teens…this paperback will be a favorite among young adults and earns itself a 5 rating."

—*Lane Education Service District* (5 out of 5 Stars)

The Book of Michael

"Without descending into stock problem-solving or rote moralizing, Michael's mentors provide commentary regarding acceptance and change."

—*Kirkus*

"Examining redemption and re-assimilation, Choyce's sober style rewards readers."

—*School Library Journal*